The Small Town Cowboy

The Texas Matchmakers of Mule Hollow are at it again! Love happens at its own pace and for Izzy and Luc, they've got singing angels helping the Matchmakin' Posse—it's literally a match made from heaven...

It's been eight years since hairstylist Lacy Brown drove into town in her ancient pink Cadillac and set the town on the map. Now, she's hired a new stylist, Izzy Cranberry, who is happy to be in the town that's made history with its everlasting "Wives Wanted Campaign" that is still running even now. But she's not looking, she's just intrigued by her two sweet grandmothers who've followed the story of Mule Hollow from the beginning until they took their last breaths and left her to fulfill their dream of moving to the tiny town for them... Unable to disappoint them, she's here—but not for long. Just to let her grams watch from above as she joins Lacy Brown Matlock in Heavenly Inspirations fixing hair—*not* being a match made by the Matchmakers of Mule Hollow.

Styling is all she's here for…and maybe a laugh or two from the legendary matchmakers who sit in her styling chair and think they have her on their target board.

Horse trainer Luc Asher has taken a job in the town he's heard a lot about but has no plan to be one of the "matches". He's a loner, with good reason, and as far from looking for love as a man can get.

Making him the perfect target…at least that's what Esther Mae, Norma Sue, and Adela, the town matchmakers, believe the moment he strides into Sam's Diner looking as handsome and alone as a man shouldn't be.

Let the fun begin in this new series set in the all-time favorite town of Mule Hollow, Texas, where the "Wives Wanted Campaign" lives on…

THE TROUBLE WITH A SMALL TOWN COWBOY

Texas Matchmakers At It Again, Book One

DEBRA CLOPTON

THE TROUBLE WITH A SMALL TOWN COWBOY

Copyright © 2023 Debra Clopton Parks

CHAPTER ONE

Mule Hollow is the place to be. The words played in Izzy Cranberry's brain as she pushed open the back door, yawned and walked out onto the porch of the house she was renting in Mule Hollow, Texas.

The town her grams loved.

She smiled as the bright morning sun shined down on the small house like a spotlight from heaven as her beloved Gram and Grammy, watched her first morning in the place they'd wanted her to visit for them.

So here she was, just for them.

The two entertaining ladies had even made up a song about her visiting the town and sang it to her many times over the last years of their lives. The last years where she was there beside them, taking care of them like they'd done for her when she'd needed them so early in her life.

Izzy's great-grandmother, Gram as she called her, passed away at the age of one-hundred-and-six-years young. It was still hard to believe the dear lady had lived that long. Her grandmother, who Izzy called Grammy, lived two years longer and was eighty-seven when she'd entered the gates of heaven. Izzy smiled thinking about the fun those two, the amazing mother and daughter team had brought into her life. She knew they were doing the same up in Heaven, where they'd joined her mom and dad, who had beat them all. Her mom had been thirty-nine and her dad forty when she'd been born and they'd called her their-dream-come-true.

They'd died together three years after she'd been born. And so, her life with Grammy had begun. She'd raised Izzy with the help of Gram, who had come to live with them when Izzy was ten. The two devoted ladies had been wonderful for Izzy.

Her blue-eyed grams, who called her their blue-eyed treasure, had taken wonderful care of her. They'd been determined to give her all their love and the love that her parents hadn't been able to do on earth.

She smiled thinking about it. They'd done a lot of that through their love of songs, bringing light and happiness to her—by changing up the lyrics to point straight at her.

Those two still carried on singing in her head and heart as clearly as if they were still alive. And they were singing right now, in their slightly off-tuned voices the song they'd loved—and created—because of their dream of her moving to Mule Hollow. The little town that had been made well-known across the country by three older ladies, the Matchmakers of Mule Hollow and the younger Lacy Brown Matlock. And her grams had come up with words to a song that was playing in her head right now. Words they'd applied to the tune of their favorite television show, *Green Acres*…

Mule Hollow is the place to be.

The small town where your dreams—come true!

A special cowboy waits for you…

In Mule Hollow, oh yes.

She chuckled: the lyrics weren't exactly right and the tune was off a bit, but it was fun listening and watching her grams singing together for her. And she still heard them singing many lyrics of their own making to that tune...

Now, she was here. Actually here in Mule Hollow and she could feel them smiling hugely and singing their hearts out just for her.

And her smile was huge as she carried her mug of hot coffee out onto the back porch of the house she'd rented. The house she'd been unable to believe she was able to rent. Lacy Brown Matlock's house. The place where it all began.

She was up now at sunrise, and it didn't matter that she'd arrived here long after midnight as she was always an early riser. That too, came from her grams. This morning was no different, she was up and dressed for her first morning jog on the country dirt road. But coffee called first. It wasn't even seven in the morning—which for her was normally late however, yesterday had been long as she'd finished up packing, then saying goodbye to long-time neighbors before finally driving across Texas to fulfill Gram and Grammy's dream.

Not completely fill their dream, but most of it, then

she would decide for the first time in her life where her next move was going to be. Her real move to the large city where she would start over with *her* dream. But for now, she was here in Mule Hollow to give her sweet grandmothers a view from heaven of the place they would have loved to visit but never made it to.

The town that had a wild history of matchmakin' from the day the three older ladies put an ad in newspapers across Texas trying to save their dying town. An old oil and ranching town that lost most of its residents when the oil boom in the area busted. Everyone left except for the cowboys and a few others, but the town was dying. Then the ads came out: Mule Hollow—wives needed.

And history was made as the stylist Lacy Brown saw the ad, loaded up her old pink topless caddy with a suitcase and her best friend, manicurist Sheri Marsh, and they'd come to town to help Lacy's mission come true—while helping the matchmakers when the ladies started answering the ad.

Lacy had said they would be coming to town in search of love, and Lacy would be there to style their hair, help match them up and share her love of Jesus with them. And history was made as she'd been doing just that. Izzy's grandmothers had followed the trip through the now-famous Molly Popp's weekly articles.

And those articles were where her grams and everyone else began following the escapades of the Matchmakin' Posse as they were called...

Those escapades helped her sweet grams, who were not as healthy as they needed to be, smile, laugh, and have fun every time the paper arrived on Saturday. They'd read Molly's newspaper post ever since the articles first started, maybe eleven years or more. Now, Izzy was here for them—not to find love, just to live for a few months in the place that brought her grams joy over the last few years of their lives.

Izzy had decided she had to see it for them—and she might as well work while she was here too. She was a hairstylist too, and Lacy had hired her over the phone after hearing why she wanted to move to town. She'd also made this cute house part of the deal.

Now, with her hand holding the large coffee mug, she managed to pull the door closed behind herself then turned and stopped short as her gaze took in the view of the blue hillside.

"Whoa, wow…*amazing,*" the words tumbled out as she stared in awe at the hillside of Texas bluebonnets stretching before her.

The *entire* hillside glowed with the morning sunshine on the bluebonnets like sapphire water cascading down the huge rolling hillside, small white waves at each peak.

Stunned, she sank into the porch swing and took a sip of coffee as tears filled her eyes. "Oh, *Grams,* you would be so thrilled to see this," she gasped in awe, then realized her grams were seeing it from up above.

She sighed, relishing the joy in that moment—she'd made the right move coming here. It was worth it for this single moment in time.

"Move to Mule Hollow," Gram had said. *"It's wonderful and you'll have fun and hopefully fall in love with one of those gorgeous cowboys."*

Izzy wasn't looking for a gorgeous cowboy or any man right now. She simply felt a strong pull to change her life, to start over.

She couldn't shake the draw of fulfilling her two grandmothers' dream of at least visiting Mule Hollow. Add to that, she was a hairstylist, and one call to Lacy and she was hired.

Lacy had been ecstatic. "Yes, yes, please come. Izzy Cranberry, *you're* the answer to my prayers!"

The thrilled reply told Izzy that for now, she'd made the right choice. Lacy had two children now, and though she had wonderful daycare here in town for them, she would love a little more time off to be a mom. And the fact that she'd followed the town story with her grams gave Izzy the background needed.

"So," Lacy had said with more enthusiasm than Izzy expected. "You will fit right in. You're the—" she'd paused then added quickly, "—*new talent in town.*"

She'd made sure Lacy knew that for now, she was temporary, simply taking a break before deciding what she wanted out of life.

And this morning she was surrounded by bluebonnets...and they were calling her name. She stood up, set her coffee on the porch table and jogged down the two steps, glad she was already in her running shoes, jogging shorts, and T-shirt.

At the barbed wire fence, she didn't hesitate, bent over and slipped through the fence and into the pasture. Instantly a huge smile burst to her lips as freedom shot through her, a release she'd needed. She began walking uphill into the mass of thick bountiful surges of blue— the Texas state flowers were breathtaking. Especially close-up.

The blue was amazing, gently waving in the wind, like her wavy hair that was also playing in the breeze. A strand slapped her across the face, and she chuckled as she pushed it away, while taking her next step in the thick blue mass of flowers—she breathed in the air, enjoyed the fresh air as her foot dipped back down into the flowers and froze as the distinct sound of a rattlesnake filled the air.

Heart pounding as her gaze shot to the ground in front of her searching through the dense flowers. Her throat and mouth went dry, her heart freaked out as two feet away, off to the side, she spotted the coiled-up rattlesnake, head lifted as it glared at her.

Oh, Lord, she gasped an internal prayer and in that same instant out of the corner of her eye she caught movement on the hilltop. Her gaze shifted from the horrifying snake ready to strike to the cowboy sitting in the saddle of his horse as he topped the blue hill's ridge.

"Help," she silently cried out, knowing he was too far away to help her before this rattler struck her leg.

Should I dive off to the side?

The thought hit her as the cowboy instantly pulled his rifle from the long sheath attached to his saddle, lifted it and aimed.

Aimed!

Heart stampeding, she had a rattlesnake beside her and a cowboy with a rifle aimed, hopefully, at the snake and not her. She stood frozen, praying God was working in her favor.

And then the shot rang out...

CHAPTER TWO

Luc Asher's Brahman bull had broken through the fence to roam, so he'd ridden across the pastures searching for the temperamental animal. He topped the hill overlooking the small pink house that had been vacant since before he arrived in town.

Lacy Matlock, the owner, was waiting for the perfect fit—her words not his—then added that she'd know the right one when God gave her the tap on the shoulder. He'd thought it funny.

But the woman was one lady who listened to the Lord, and everyone in town told him so when he'd arrived a few weeks ago. His friend and reason for being here, Pace, had said the same thing.

And the stories of Mule Hollow proved it.

All these thoughts happened quickly as his gaze swept to the house sitting there waiting—empty as usual—suddenly, a golden-haired female snagged his attention. She stood frozen halfway down the hill in the thick mass of bluebonnets, and her frozen, alarmed gaze locked onto his, then returned to the ground near her.

Instantly his instinct kicked in, and he ripped his gaze from her, knowing why she stood frozen. He scanned the ground as he drew his rifle from its holster. Spotting the rattlesnake, head up, ready to strike—thank goodness they didn't always strike instantly but gave a rattling warning. Luc had time as he'd automatically, with no hesitation, lifted the rifle he always carried loaded and ready for a meetup with a rattlesnake or any other surprise he might run into. Thankfully, they weren't seen as often as believed, but it only took one run-in to know to be prepared.

The smart woman remained frozen. Horrified eyes connected to his, but as she saw him raise his rifle, the glint in her eyes was steady, she shot to her left and then back at him. It was all he needed to know—if she was going to make a dive it would be away from the rattler.

Away from his shot—so he nodded and pulled the trigger as she dove the opposite way.

The bullet hit its target, and on impact the large rattlesnake blew into the air, writhing as it flew. And the blonde-haired beauty hit the ground then stood up and raced toward the house as fast as those bootless feet and bare legs would carry her.

He shoved his rifle back into its sheath, nudged Magnum, and the horse charged down the hill and caught up to the woman as she reached the fence near the house. She gripped the wooden fence post, gasping as she looked up at him with eyes glowing with relief. Eyes that matched the bluebonnets surrounding them.

"Are you alright?" He hopped from his horse, giving gratitude to God who had prepared him to be there in this woman's time of need. This beautiful woman hooked him with her smile as her wide, soft lips lifted.

"Thanks to you, I'm good. But I don't know how I'd have been if you hadn't miraculously come over that hill. I wasn't thinking and just walked out into the beautiful bluebonnets—I didn't remember to be careful," she said, her words harsh. "Even from the city, I was taught to be careful, but was I—*no*. I walked off into these beauties with no thought except to enjoy this sapphire hillside."

Even upset she had a way with words that he liked. He saw why Lacy Brown Matlock must have decided she was perfect for her pink house—or maybe he just saw what he wanted to see. The house with its dangling, sparkling glass chimes and the glistening metal wind chimes that even now, since the trauma was gone, he could hear singing in the breeze fit this woman.

The cowboys of Mule Hollow are going to compete for this lady. Your neighbor—

Pushing the choir blaring in his brain away, he held out his hand, needing to calm her down—or himself. "Hi, I'm glad I was here. I'm Luc Asher, your neighbor down the road. You must be Lacy's new tenant." That smile widened, and she took his hand and instantly fire shot through him.

"Yes, I am," she said, her voice raspy from fear and running—maybe from their hands connecting. "I'm Izzy Cranberry. The new resident of that cute little pink house."

He grinned and forced himself to release her hand. "That's what I assumed. There's never anyone else out here when I come checking cattle or riding horses. Lacy has been…" He should not say it, but he did, "She's been looking for someone to rent that spot, and she found you."

"Well, I actually found her, and she was nice enough to rent me this place—and thankfully because of you, I'll be able to enjoy it and tell her how much I love the bluebonnets—well, I did. Still do, but I'll admire them from afar. I won't be walking among them again."

"If you want to go walking, pull on a pair of boots, a pair that comes right below your knees, but as small as you are, a regular pair should do. From a cowboy's standpoint, you can do anything in a pair of cowboy boots—" Her eyes went to her feet. His followed, down her small, pretty frame. It was obvious she worked out. Her thin legs had the bulge of muscles, shapely—he yanked his gaze back up before she caught him staring. She looked up, not seeing that his gaze had strayed, he'd make sure he didn't do it again.

"I'll get a pair." Her voice and gaze were serious now.

"Jogging a long way might get old, but you can walk up this flowery hillside and through the grassy pastures this time of year with no worries. I ride every day on one of the horses, but today I'm looking for a bull. I don't think he would have attacked you, but he's big and might have startled you. He knocked a fence down."

"He could have been what was after me instead of the rattlesnake? Whoa, I hadn't thought of all of this. I'm from the city, and I'm only here because of my gram—no, because *I* needed a change. Gram has always followed the Molly Popp articles on Mule Hollow cowboys—you know what I mean since you're from here."

"Yes," he said with a laugh. "I know exactly what you mean. I have to say, from what my friend Pace says—he married Sheri, who was in that pink Cadillac with Lacy when she drove into town—things can get out of control quickly. He's happy it did for him, but he warned me in case I wasn't expecting the posse to come after me. And I'm not."

Her brows hitched above brighter eyes. "From what my gram said, they come after everyone—but I'm not on the market either. Sheri and Pace live nearby?"

"When they're in town they live at their new house further down the road where I've taken over the original small house. I'm here looking after his cattle and breaking horses while he and Sheri are out in Australia training some folks there on breaking horses our way—" Why was he going into detail? It was *not* his way.

"So, we may be in the same boat." He grinned.

"As the story goes, yes. But I figure when that time comes, I'll be ready, but right now falling in love is my call, not theirs." She smiled big and bright at her words, and it dug deep and nudged at his heart.

"I'm here because of my grandmother. I'm a hairstylist and love my career. But my gram got sick and had no one but me, so I dropped my career and went to be with her. From the very beginning she read every article written by Molly Popp—I know her name now is different but Popp kind of *pops*, so they left it that way on the articles. Gram and Grammy dreamed of moving out here, then Gram got bedridden, not uncommon for someone over a hundred. She lay in that bed for four years. I moved home to be with her and got brought up to date with each story. So, I have to personally thank her, Lacy, and Sheri, and many more for being part of the smile that was always on Gram's face even when she was in pain."

It never ended, these people who had stories of how Mule Hollow had helped them. He knew this had to have meant a lot to this obviously sweet lady. Her love for her two grandmothers showed in her eyes.

In the distance, there was a loud, very loud bellow of a bull. Thankfully something to switch his brain off this beauty and put him back to work. He spun, and there, standing on the hill, was the huge white and black bull with a large hump on his back.

"Is that the one they call a Brahman bull, with the hump?"

He grinned. "You got it. They are usually calm and likable. Mammoth wasn't raised the right way and is now one irritable bull. But I like him, so I'm working with him to get him happy again."

In that instant the bull let out a loud "What are you doing here" bellow, and beside him Izzy laughed—it was like the sound of an ever-twinkling wind chime. He looked at her. Goodness the woman sparkled, she wasn't afraid anymore and it showed. She looked like a bright light among the bluebonnets.

"He sounds very gentle," she teased.

He laughed. "Better than that rattler. I'll leave you now." He tipped his hat, ready to get away. "Get you some boots so you don't have to worry next time you're walking up this hill."

"I'll get some boots, but seriously doubt I'll be back on this hill. If I decide to learn how to ride a horse, I'll ride one and put the distance of a stirrup and the ground between me and the snakes. *And* add a pair of boots too."

"I'm down the road there, at the end. You can't miss me, so if you want to ride a horse, come see me. I promise I know what I'm doing. I train them, and when I'm finished, they're calm, no beating involved in how I break a horse. I promise you, if there is a horse you can get on and ride safely, it's mine."

He wasn't bragging. It was the truth, and he knew it. It was also time to go. He grabbed the horn of his saddle, stuck one boot in the stirrup and then he settled into the saddle and grinned down at her. "Be careful going to the house, and don't run into one of those twinkling glass or metal chimes hanging from the trees because you're studying the ground looking for another snake. I'll see you later." He turned his horse and with one click of his knee, they were off—instantly Mammoth let out a bellow and charged the other way.

Racing up the hill, Luc was unable to stop himself from glancing over his shoulder one more time at the pretty Izzy Cranberry looking bright and shiny in the sunlight as she watched him ride.

He yanked his gaze away and concentrated on his ride. But despite everything telling him not to—he was looking forward to the next time he saw her again.

He also knew, whether she was looking or not, when the matchmakers met her, she was in for a ride. A matchmaking ride that, from what he'd heard, might be harder to avoid than that rattlesnake had been.

CHAPTER THREE

Izzy had just gotten back to the house when suddenly the amazing pink Cadillac whipped into her driveway. Behind the wheel was the blonde-headed, grinning Lacy Brown Matlock. As soon as the car halted, she sprang up from the seat to sit on the door. Then she swung her legs from inside to outside and hopped to the ground all in a matter of seconds.

"Howdy, it is *grrreat* to see you, Izzy Cranberry. With that name and that smile, you fit with the house and the town like whip cream topping on berry cobbler—a match made in heaven." And then Lacy gave her a welcoming hug.

Izzy laughed. This had been the oddest day, one full of delight, fear and gratitude and now laughter—and not to be left out, a handsome cowboy to the rescue.

Not that she was interested, the cowboy had saved her from a rattlesnake making him hard to ignore. But now, she was staring at the one and only Lacy Brown and her pink caddy. This day was definitely one to remember.

"Grammy and her mother, Gram, would be so excited right now—I take that back—they *are* excited watching from up above."

"That's so touching. Molly's articles have brought many ladies to our town looking for love. We still run the ads in rotation in several areas of Texas, and they still bring ladies to town to meet our cowboys. And sometimes find love."

"Gram loved it and always read it to me."

Lacy's amazing smile radiated from her, as did her dazzling blue eyes. "Wonderful," she said. "I'm so thankful we gave your grandmas something to enjoy. Now, are you ready for a ride?"

Izzy's gaze shot to the famous car. "In your caddy? Your pink caddy?"

Lacy hooted. "*Yeah,* I want to give you a tour of your new hometown, and there's nothing like riding in my topless pink Cadillac—that's where it started for me."

Izzy grinned hearing the lyrics to the old Jerry Lee Lewis song "Pink Cadillac" playing in her mind. Her gram had enjoyed the song, though she'd warned Izzy to never get in the back of a pink Cadillac. Izzy hadn't understood until she'd listened to the song when she was older and got it. Now it just made her smile, thinking how they were trying to protect her.

"My grandmothers would be happy, and that's why I'm here. So, a ride in the pink caddy is perfect."

Lacy tapped her long, sparkling pink fingernails— things her grams talked about too—and it was clear now as she watched those fingernails tap on the hood of that pink caddy that Molly Popp had a way with words because in that moment everything was coming alive.

"Let's do this. Although I'm not going to hop into it just yet like you do. But one day I'll give it a try, but I don't want to start the trip with a broken leg or a broken nose. Today I've pushed the limits with an angry bull and a rattlesnake, so I'll pass jumping over the caddy's door." She laughed: it was true.

Lacy slapped one hand on the door and vaulted over

it and into the seat like it was an easy thing to do. Having kids had not stopped this lady's agility. "Hop in and tell me where you met an angry bull and a rattlesnake this morning."

She hadn't meant to say that, but she got into the car through the open door and looked over at the questioning eyes of Lacy. "Actually, just now. I went through the fence to see the beautiful hillside of bluebonnets and halfway up the hill I met a rattlesnake. Thank goodness that horse trainer Luc Asher came riding over the hill chasing a runaway bull. He saw me frozen, and goodness, he pulled his rifle out and within seconds that rattler was flying through the air. Me, I raced down the hill, and he and his horse caught me at the fence, and we introduced ourselves."

There, she'd gotten it all out, but she saw a flash in Lacy's blue eyes. Eyes that were now glued on Izzy. "That's awesome."

"Yes, it was. Because then I heard a loud bellow and looked up. On the top of the hill stood a huge angry bull—the bull that had brought the cowboy to my rescue."

Lacy reached out and patted her shoulder.

"Welcome to Mule Hollow. We have rattlesnakes, big bulls, lots of cows, sweet little baby calves, and Samantha, our matchmaking donkey. I'm sure you'll meet her soon. And…" She paused, her eyes sparkling like a mass of stars in a navy sky. "And you've met your first cowboy. A *real* cowboy who saved the day. We've got lots of cowboys if he's not the one."

Lacy's words slammed into Izzy. She'd said way too much. They needed to get the message that she was looking for her new life, *her* life that she'd paused to watch over her wonderful grandmothers. Gram and Grammy.

She'd never been unhappy about that, but now, she was looking for the life she wanted. Of course, she'd started here, at the place they'd always loved.

"Yes, I met him, and I'm happy to meet more cowboys, but I need to let you know, that's all I'm here for. I'm not here to fall in love."

Lacy laughed as she cranked the caddy, gunned the engine, then shifted the gear, all in a split second, and then they blasted backwards as she locked eyes on Izzy. "Girlfriend, I was the same way. But when God's got a plan, He's got a plan. So, get ready, I'm not your matchmaker, God is. I'm just the one who likes to watch and play off of what I see."

She sat there as they whipped out of the drive backward. Lacy shifted into drive, and in a flash, they shot down the road. She instantly put her seat belt on because, whoa baby, Lacy Brown Matlock liked to put the peddle to the metal in this pink caddy and, as old as it was, it was all cranked up. A 1957 Cadillac that still had fire because somebody obviously kept it in great shape.

And now, she was having the ride of her life as they zoomed down the road to an Elvis Presley song blasting from the radio—"All Shook Up"—and she was, in more ways than one.

This was going to be an adventure.

They whizzed down the road and once they turned down the main road again and out from under the roads of oaks and hills and hit the long straightaway that led to town, there in the distance sat Mule Hollow. Just like she'd been told by Gram. *Amazing*. Even this far away, Lacy's famous pink hair salon, Heavenly Inspirations, stood out like it was calling for them to come to town. And it was surrounded by the rainbow colors of the other businesses running on each side of the road.

"Enjoy the ride, I love it. I've always found joy behind the wheel of this caddy. When I'm having problems or trying to hear God's words of wisdom, I find it while I'm driving. How about you?"

She smiled, loving the feel of the wind on her face, and she realized in those few minutes, she'd relaxed. "I feel what you're saying. It's like the breeze is clearing my heart and mind." She suddenly teared up. "Oh, Lacy, I feel my sweet grams smiling right now."

Lacy beamed at her. "Yep, yep, yep, there's power in the feel of the air and the blue sky above and the sunlight shining down on you. I'm so glad you know your grams are happy you're here. I'll tell you a secret, at night with the moonlight shining down on you, it's even stronger. I always love riding at night."

Lacy had her eyes back on the road, but Izzy had her gaze on the amazing lady. She now understood the draw of this blonde firecracker of a woman, she knew how to help someone feel what they needed. She'd needed a ride, the feel of the air on her skin and the shining light of hope that surrounded her as she took it all in.

"You're going to love meeting the gang at Sam's. They're all there waiting on us. I told them that you might be tired or not ready, but they said they wanted to meet you and whether you showed up or not, they'd be there waiting."

"I'm looking forward to meeting them. Again, sweet gram felt like she was one of them. She loved hearing of their escapades."

Lacy hooted. "Oh, yes, they have those! But more than that, they cause escapades to happen to others. So, be on the lookout because they may instigate an escapade for you."

She laughed at the thought. Izzy hoped not since she wasn't looking for their kind of romantic escapade, but the idea, she knew, had Gram smiling. Probably hoping and praying she did have one—suddenly, handsome Luc Asher's face flashed into her thoughts. She yanked her thoughts from the romantic jaunt and focused on the town.

Focused on the yellow building across the road from the pink salon. Then the blue store, the green store, so many different colors she felt like it was a bright rainbow resting at the end of the road. She knew one was a candy store, one a dress store, a feed store, a sheriff's office, a real-estate office, and a Prickly Pear Jelly store her grams had wanted to see. And of course, Sam's Diner—and there it was. It had a few tables outside on the wide sidewalk where she knew, from her articles, Popp had sat there and worked. The town was bright and inviting, and she smiled at the sight.

"I feel like I've been here before. Just listening to Gram read me the articles from her bed all the time, and then me reading them to her when she no longer had the strength. It's amazing."

Lacy pulled into a slot in front of the diner. "I love hearing stories about your grandmothers. They knew us all from the beginning, the moment I drove into town for the first time. Everyone has aged just a tad, but praise the Lord, we're all still here. We really have a great time, and there's still a lot of cowboys who need wives." She grinned. "And that's the name of the game."

Izzy tried not to let the look in Lacy's eyes put tension in her gut. But those dancing bluebird eyes couldn't be ignored. "I guess I better get out," she said. She opened her door and stepped out.

Lacy slid up and onto the door before jumping to

the ground. "Yep, yep, yep, let's go inside before they stampede out to meet you. So, now, let's give your grams a treat while they watch from above as we go into the diner and I introduce you to everyone."

They both stepped up onto the wooden planked sidewalk. The sign said Sam's Diner, and she was grinning as Lacy opened the door and she stepped inside.

Wow. Just wow, it was old but amazing. So far everything had been amazing. And as the door opened, she could hear the jukebox playing and the famous singer Jerry Lee Lewis singing, *Great Balls of Fire*…as if her grams had picked it, and she suddenly hoped she wasn't about to step into trouble.

Then again, that might just make her grams chuckle.

CHAPTER FOUR

The walls were old rough wood. It was old and wonderful and seemed to say hello.

Three ladies sat in a booth against the wall, and they waved—she knew them instantly. Adela Ledbetter Green with her sweet look, her short white hair that swept about the edges of her dainty face in an excellent cut. Beside her, a grinning Esther Mae Wilcox with her colored red hair waved. Her eyes as bright as her hair and her smile. And then there on the opposite side of the table was the bulky, overall-clad Norma Sue Jenkins. She was almost the first to hop from the booth, but in that moment out from the two swinging doors of the diner came small, bowlegged cowboy Sam. There was no denying who each one was as her grams had described them and showed her pictures of all of them that had made it into the newspaper or magazine articles through the years. Her grams kept them all.

She glanced around the room and saw the two checker players who were sitting by the window, their gazes locked on her. Applegate Thornton and Stanley Orr, and it didn't take anything for her to know which was which. Her gram had always smiled as she'd talked about the two older men.

Applegate was skinny as a rail, tall, and had a face full of lines and eyes that hid beneath his bushy brows. Then there was Stanley Orr, a little more weight, a softer look to his round face, and a kind look in his eyes as they both stared at her.

"Glad you're here," Applegate grunted, not sounding pleased, but she knew he hid his feelings with his growls and hidden eyes.

"Shor are," Stanley chimed in, his eyes glowing. "Come join us in a game of checkers one day. We're gonna leave you alone right now cuz the ladies have been waitin' and excited about this moment," Stanley finished as he looked back at the checkerboard, grinned, and jumped his red chip over App's black checker.

Applegate yelped, "You take that back. It's my turn."

She almost chuckled out loud at the antics that Gram loved.

Lacy leaned close. "They haven't changed."

Sam was beside them now, he looked up at her—didn't have to look up too far because she was short too. "Howdy, alrighty, you've met Applegate and Stanley and one day you might come in and play with them just to give them a challenge. But right now, I have to tell you that my sweet Adela and her two buddies have been anticipatin' meeting you ever since Lacy told them she'd hired you. But," he leaned in, "I honestly need to warn you that it has nothing to do with you coming to help in the salon. There're other things involved, and if you've heard about Mule Hollow, you know exactly what I'm warning you about." He held his hand out.

Oh, goodness, she stared at that hand, she'd heard about his famous handshake and tried to prepare herself as she lifted hers to his. His large, rough hand gripped hers in a handshake like she'd never had before. It was tight, and he shook it up and down hard, as if trying to lift her whole body up and slap it to the ground.

Goodness gracious—"Great Balls of Fire"—the song came *back* on the jukebox loud and clear and thank goodness she didn't yelp.

The man had not lost his touch since Molly first described it in her newspaper article. Grammy said it was legendary. That Sam had a grip that could take you to your knees if you made him mad. Thank the good Lord she hadn't made him mad and didn't intend to. But her gaze instantly flew to the ladies, who were all grinning because they obviously enjoyed watching newbies get a shake—or a take down from Sam.

Finally, Sam released her hand as if nothing had happened, grinned and said, "Welcome to Mule Hollow. Now follow me."

Mule Hollow is the place to be... Her grams sang in her spinning brain as she followed tiny *superman* Sam to the table.

It suddenly hit her that she knew why she was here, but she had no idea what was coming.

And that suddenly made her nervous.

With his new neighbor on his mind, Luc drove out to

34

Clint Matlock's ranch. The town's annual rodeo event was going to happen at the end of the week, and they were finalizing the details. It wasn't like he was one of the long-standing friends who would be at the meeting. But he was filling in until his friend Pace got back from Australia. Luc was Pace's stand-in and trying hard to fit in.

He liked everybody. Clint Matlock was a great cowboy—a ranch owner who knew his business and ran a fantastic well-known ranch. Bob Jacobs had a ranch he'd opened up a few years back, and the big guy was doing well. Most of the ranchers in town were, as well as the cowboys who worked the massive ranches surrounding this small town.

These cowboys knew their business, and what they didn't know they learned from their buddies. Pace had told him exactly that, but the one thing about Luc that he'd learned from life experience was you had to build your own opinions of people, good or bad. You had to put up your own roadblocks of who you let in and who you locked out. Sitting there in the saddle of a bucking bull was a challenge he no longer took. He controlled his life and never planned to let a bull or anything else control it again.

His past hurt was never-ending in its endurance, and though he'd gone to Idaho and hid out for a long time, it was still with him. And always would be. He just had to find a new way to deal with it.

Pace had reached out to offer a hand. He'd met Pace on the huge Idaho ranch the year before Pace left the ranch of solitude. He'd taken the Lord as his Savior and felt drawn to leave the isolation and be among people again. Mix and mingle and not hide in the seclusion of the huge ranch they worked. The loner was taking God's lead and stepping out.

At the ranch, they spent the worst part of the winters holed up on part of the property, a cowboy and a herd of cattle he was responsible for were isolated. A cowboy with a medical saddle bag for emergencies that he had to take care of and a silent campfire he sat alone at if the weather permitted.

For some reason, Pace had called him at least twice a year to check on him, and he always invited him to Mule Hollow. Then this last time, something in him wouldn't let himself say no. It was as if there was a wrench twisting inside of him holding back the word no.

So here he was, but, like Pace had told him, it was time for a new start. Time to walk away from the past and find a new life like he had.

Like he had.

Not exactly what Luc was looking for. He wasn't looking for another woman in his life. He had learned from a wrong, rough experience that it didn't matter if something pulled his heartstrings, he wasn't getting involved again.

Nope, nada, not happening. He was a loner, and he might not be hiding out on the back end of a huge ranch in the Idaho backcountry anymore, but that didn't mean he was jumping into anything other than training horses.

His heart was closed no matter how much of a matchmaking community this was, despite that he liked the town. Mule Hollow was an intriguing community. The wide range of ladies and kids and happy cowboy spouses was great. The checker players at Sam's Diner were fun. Applegate Thornton and Stanley Orr were funny fellows to watch, listen and play checkers with.

Those two liked to eye everyone, measure them up and guess who was the next victim of the Posse.

They were eyeing him, and he knew it. But they were going to be disappointed. He was still playing with them if he had time and knew that they were wondering if he was ever going to notice any special lady who came to town.

He just laughed internally about it. One thing was for certain about him—when he made his mind up about something, nothing was changing it.

Nothing.

He'd learned some pain never left, and it wasn't happening ever again to him.

He shut his brain down as he drove down the long drive of Clint Matlock's ranch; he'd inherited it from his dad but had helped build it from a young age. It was a well-known ranch across the country. He saw the trucks of Zane Cantrell, who was married to prickly pear jelly maker Rose—the lady and their son Max made some great jelly out of a flowering cactus. Then there was Dan Dawson, married to the dress store owner Ashby. Then Cort Wells, a great horse trainer who judged horses around the world and was married to Lilly—the owner of the very much-loved donkey, Samantha. That fat little donkey was a draw to the town events almost as much as the single cowboys—him not included. He focused on what he was doing, helping plan a rodeo today.

He was the last one here, so he shut the engine off and hopped from the truck and headed for the barn. Inside he found everyone standing near a stall. And there was a brand-new colt.

"He's a good-lookin' fella," he said and meant it. It was obvious the tiny fella came from great stock.

Cort Wells held out his hand in welcome. "Glad you could join us." They shook hands and then both put their hands back on their hips. "You'll enjoy this experience. All of us..." He grinned and looked around the group. "We're all wondering how you'll react when the matchmakers put their eyes on you. We'll be watching, and if you need any help, just ask us. We all fumbled around and figured things out, and you will too."

Bob cocked his head to the side and crossed his

arms. "And if you're like me, they make the wrong match sometimes. Their first shot isn't always right. Don't get to thinking that just because the matchmakers have their eyes on you that they're going to pick the right one on their first target."

The fellas were all grinning. He was frowning. "Y'all are acting like Applegate, Stanley, and Sam—though Sam is quiet about it in his own way. That man's eyes take in everything. But App and Stanley put it out there while I was playing checkers with them and told me that I would be on the radar. I'm not planning to be on the radar."

Clint leveled his gaze. "Well, cowboy, sometimes it doesn't matter what you want or are looking for. If you get on the radar, it's hard to get off of it. But until the right woman comes along, it won't help anyone. So anyway, let's get off the subject of this developing cowboy romance and the not-ready-to-love portion which we've all been-there-felt-that and know it all worked out for our best. Now let's focus on why we're here."

This was crazy. They were all grinning and had

knowing looks in their eyes.

"Hold on," Deputy Zane Cantrell said. "Even your buddy Pace would tell you that sometimes you just have to let things happen. When the right one comes along it might not always feel right or the timing is off. But the perfect match—if it's meant to be, I wouldn't let it pass by."

"I'm glad I'm going to be entertaining to all of you, but I'm sorry to tell y'all that the entertainment is only going to go so far. Now, like Clint said, let's get back to why we're here—the rodeo. I've never been, so y'all tell me about it. What's the best thing you've seen since it started?"

Dan instantly chuckled. "Well, we're having the greased pig hustle this year. They don't always do it, but the ladies are the ones that request some of the things and the first year it ever happened I watched my Ashby—she wasn't mine at the time—but them gals got her out there trying to tackle a greased-up pig and it was quite fun to watch. Of course, at that time there was nothing between us, but when I look back on it, watching that city gal out there trying to catch that wild, running, greased pig, it still stands in my memory. So, we're doing it again and who knows, you might see someone out there trying to catch a greased pig running wild and next thing you know you've got yourself a happily-ever-after."

Whoa—what was wrong with these guys? He forced a grin. "That does sound like an entertaining moment, but nothing is going to come of it with me." A short laugh escaped despite everything as he pictured the women trying to tackle a greased, fat pig. "They are little pigs, right?" he asked.

"Yep, fast critters," Bob said.

"Okay, so it does sound entertaining." He couldn't help adding because it was true.

"You'll find," Clint said, clapping him on the back, "that remark comes often here in our tiny town. So now, let's get the meeting started to finish up everything for this weekend."

And so, the meeting began. They followed Clint into his large office. From what Luc had heard, he had this one for meetings with his cowhands and things like this. But he had an office inside too, for his office work.

It was nice, something that suddenly slammed into Luc might be a goal worth having…a home to call his own, a business, and a fam—he shut that thought down. *No.*

He looked around. He was a trainer, a cattleman. He looked over cattle and doctored them when he was out in the middle of a huge ranch snowed in and doing his job.

He was good at what he did, but the best thing he was good at was breaking a horse in a good way. He never hit them, spurred them or whipped them. He just used his hands, his halter, lead rope, and long pole used to direct them, guide them with a touch. It was a magical thing and he enjoyed it—yeah, he enjoyed being in control.

Peaceful control.

And that was how he trained his horses. And that was the way he'd keep his life.

As he sat down and began listening to them talk about the rodeo and the fun times they were preparing for all the people who would come from all over to see for themselves here in the small town of Mule Hollow, he was fascinated.

But as he sat there, his crazy mind went back to that smiling woman. Izzy Cranberry, what a name, but she was intriguing…he shut his brain down. He wasn't looking for anything intriguing or anything like this office, this ranch—nothing that would hold him down. Nothing that would ever leave him with a heartache again.

And why that thought came up after thoughts of Izzy was confusing.

It had been a good morning meeting, but as he drove away from the ranch, instead of heading home he headed to town. It was time for lunch, and lunch at Sam's was calling his name.

He'd get back to working with his horses this afternoon. And he had a bull to check up on. He'd fixed the fence but that was one defiant bull, and if he had to, he was going to put him in a ring and work with him like he did his horses. Taming was the name of the game, even for a bull.

But himself, nope, not happening.

CHAPTER FIVE

"You are the cutest thing. I can't wait for you to work on my hair," Esther Mae said as Izzy sat down in the chair the smiling lady had pulled up to the table for her. Lacy sat down in the one they'd pulled up for her.

"I'm looking forward to it. It looks good right now, obviously you like a little fluff."

Lacy chuckled. "Yes, she does. But not nearly as fluffy as she did when I first got to town."

Esther Mae lightly patted her teased hair. "Well, like Lacy said, when she first arrived, my flaming red hair looked like a tower of red-hot coals or—like they used to say—red velvet ice cream. I thought I looked great, but Lacy told me she could give me a new look and I was all for it. I love changes—unlike Norma Sue."

Norma Sue lightly slapped her hand. "Just don't start. My hair looked great after Lacy did it, I just am not into all that curling. I've got curls of my own, no tools needed, it's just bushy. However, since Lacy sold me on those silky drops of magic that I rub in my hands, then through my hair, my frizz is gone and I have shine." She grinned a wide smile that spread across her chubby cheeks and was like a beam of sunshine.

"Yes, I agree. It looks perfect on you." It was true. The cowgirl wore her hair and red overalls like a model for a farmers and ranchers magazine.

Grinning, Lacy added, "Yes, I tried to give Norma Sue a new look, but you'll soon learn that her natural look is exactly what goes with this outgoing gal. She's like me, she is who she is, and nothing is going to change it."

"That's for certain—outspoken is the word," Esther Mae blurted out and everyone laughed.

"And *proud* of it," Norma Sue drawled, that wide grin blasted across her face again.

"They are *both* jewels in their own way," Adela

said gently. "Everyone needs a little spunk. Each of us has our own way of doing things because God works in mysterious ways and uses each of us if we let Him."

The lady was a gem, that was for certain. "You're right. But I have to say your hair fits you perfectly."

"Yeah, it's perfect and so is she," Esther Mae hooted.

"I'm not perfect," Adela said firmly. "I'm just—"

"As close as anyone can be," Norma Sue said. "We love her despite that perfection. She leads us in times when I let this sporadic Esther Mae get me off track."

Laughter ensued.

The redhead rolled her eyes. "I get excited and get words mixed up and love making matches. I'm a little spastic at times. But this gal," she pointed at Norma Sue, "she loves it." She winked at Izzy, and Izzy chuckled.

Izzy slapped a palm to her heart. "My grams are loving this. Keep going."

"These two are entertaining," Adela said, smiling. "They love helping people find a change in their life. God can use us all and them, even with their antics. And you, Izzy Cranberry, are going to be used here too."

Those sparkling blue eyes held Izzy's eyes.

She almost believed her. "I know I can help people feel better when I do their hair. I love it."

"Yes," Adela continued. "But like Lacy, you have a mission."

A mission—did she? "Yes, I'm here to live out my two grams' wishes."

"Yes, but I have a deep feeling that you're here for something too. And I know that God's using you already to help Lacy spend some more time with her lively kids."

She grinned in relief, knowing every one of the people in the room had their eyes glued on her. "Yes, I'm here because of my grams, because they both passed away before they could come for a visit. They loved y'all so much. And Molly's articles gave them joy to the end. Adela, you have a joy for God that they loved. And Esther Mae, they thought you were the funniest woman they'd ever known. Molly knew how to write you in an article like you were jumping off the pages. All of y'all's matchmaking fun was just a joy to read about and the mistakes you made were hilarious. And Norma Sue, you are one tough cookie—my gram's words." A smile spread wild. "She was restricted to her bed, but she'd be laughing so hard that she'd slap the mattress. I'd always know and ask, 'Okay, what did Norma Sue or Esther Mae do?'"

Izzy's heart tightened thinking about those wonderful moments. And now, here she was seeing the ladies in person. Everyone was laughing and her heart was filled to the limit—about to explode, and words stalled with the emotions raging through her.

"Molly is a great writer," Lacy said, grinning widely, giving her a moment. "Your grams would have loved all three of these sweet, fun ladies. I knew the day I drove into town on my mission that God had sent me here. And it was all because of the ad these three had put out in the papers. I joined them and have been blessed. We spend many hours here in Sam's Diner. Sam is wonderful too, and those two checker players have a way about them. This place, this diner, is almost exactly like it was the day I walked in. There are just more people—which is a good thing. But the jukebox still has a mind of its own, something we've all grown used to and love—even if we get irritated sometimes. But it's like life, sometimes you just can't change it. You just have to make the best of it."

As she sat there, it slammed into her that she was glad she'd come, that she'd lost her sweet grams and she was making the best of it.

Her thoughts went to the early morning and the rattler lifting its head, ready to strike. Today could have been a terrible day. But then that cowboy up on that hill met her terrified gaze, lifted his rifle and shot that rattler.

Why her mind went there, she couldn't say, but it was like now, you never knew what life was going to throw at you. You just have to change your motives sometimes, your path, and see where it leads you.

She was here to see what her grams had missed, but she was not getting involved with anyone. Even if that cowboy kept knocking on her brain's door.

In that moment, the door opened and whoever it was brought smiles to the ladies who could see the front door. She could tell by their expressions that someone interesting had entered the diner.

Norma Sue looked at her and grinned. "Now, that

is a cowboy, and you said he saved you this morning."

Her gut twisted instantly. Luc had entered the diner.

Oh, boy, now what? Her heart suddenly pounding, she shifted in her seat as she looked over her shoulder. Sam motioned to the cowboy who had removed his hat, exposing wavy black hair—wow, those sea-green eyes locked on hers as he followed Sam, who led him to the table right beside theirs.

His gaze locked onto her, and she felt like a fish caught on a hook that was flopping around on the ground trying to get back to the water. Goodness gracious—and as if somehow knowing what was playing through her brain, someone had slipped a quarter in the jukebox and Jerry Lee Lewis started singing exactly that song. *Goodness gracious, great balls of fire.* Those fireballs were slamming into her heart as he yanked his gaze off of hers, as though he'd felt the jolts too. Something told her he wasn't looking for that connection either.

"Hey, Luc," Lacy said. "How'd the meeting go out at the ranch with you and the other cowboys?"

He took the seat at the table that gave him a view of

them—probably so he could answer the question. Not so he could see her. His back to them would have been rude, and it didn't matter how much she'd wished he'd put that muscled back of his to them, he was looking straight at her.

He hooked his hat on the chair next to him. "It was good. We've got everything ready for the rodeo this weekend. This is my first one, so they had to explain things that go on to me. Like greased-up little pig catching."

The entire room erupted in laughter. Norma Sue slapped her hand on the table, shaking all their glasses.

Esther Mae hooted. "I will never forget the first time we had that. That sweet Ashby, who had never been here before, hardly ever wore jeans because she dressed so beautifully, got out there because I guess we urged her to do it. It is a memory I'll never forget. Of course, Ashby has adapted to us now, but she's still one elegant lady and that little greased-up piglet just started it all."

Luc was grinning and oh, what a grin. "I have to say from what Dan said it seemed like he had a blast, and it must have worked out since they are now married. He is one happy cowboy."

"Yep, yep, yep," Lacy sang. "Just like God works everything out. Those two found each other, a rough road that started with a greased-up pig. One never knows."

Lacy nudged Izzy, her eyes were still stuck on Luc, and now she met Lacy's gaze. "What?"

"*You* have to do that. Every woman needs to catch a pig. It's fun, and we'll get you prepared with boots, jeans, and a thick shirt. At least you'll know a little bit, unlike Ashby."

Lacy looked over at Luc. "Would you know how to teach someone how to catch a greased pig? You are one of the best horse whisperers around, so we've been told by Pace. The best."

His expression went to flat-out shock. Not about him being a world-class horse tamer, using Pace's words, but shock from the question of him helping her.

This was crazy. "No," she declared. "I'm not doing that and don't need anyone teaching me anything." She said the words and her eyes narrowed as they shot back to him.

His eyes flickered like a flame. "Why, are you chicken? You were the one who came up that hill this morning without thinking about rattlesnakes. Now they're talking about a small greased-up piglet. It's not going to be as scary or dangerous as meeting up with that rattler was—"

How dare he. "If I don't *want* to do it, I don't *want* to do it. And nothing can be as bad as meeting up with that rattlesnake."

"Then you'll do it," Esther Mae exclaimed, clapping her hands. "You're going to love it. I love watching it—though I'd never get out there these days. But I enjoy watching it just like everyone. I bet you'll catch one of those slimy little critters with or without any help. You are one tough cookie I think."

She just sat there frozen as her gaze flew about the group with expectant looks and happy smiles. Her gaze stopped on him. Suddenly she felt her grammies up in heaven laughing.

Grams *loved* reading about the pig wrestling.

She sighed, that's what she was here for. "Okay, I

came here because I'm trying to do what my grams would want to do. And they both absolutely *loved* reading about the pig wrestling. So, the message from heaven up above is I have to do this for them. I'm in."

The whole diner, including Sam, Applegate, and Stanley, went into an uproar.

How had she done this?

She had walked into it without even thinking about it. These ladies were going to try matching everyone up—suddenly it hit her, they thought she and the cowboy who was staring at her with serious, startled eyes, might very well be their next targets.

Goodness gracious, she'd walked right into that!

CHAPTER SIX

Luc woke up about five but had hardly slept at all as his mind was stuck on yesterday's diner incident. He got up and dressed, intent on getting back to horse taming—but his mind wasn't taming down either.

All he could think about was Izzy and that the ladies were trying to get him to teach her how to catch a greased pig...it was ridiculous. He couldn't teach someone how to catch a greased-up pig. He'd never done it himself.

Standing there on the dark porch with the sun just starting to peek over the trees at him, he decided he was going to town. Sam's would be open, and the ladies wouldn't be there. They were never there this early. But App and Stanley would be, grinning. He knew they'd enjoyed everything that had gone on and were wondering if he was going to fall into the trap.

No, he was not.

But he was going to say something to them and Sam. They'd lived life in Mule Hollow a lot longer than he had and maybe they could give him some advice on how to get out of this ordeal.

He reached the diner and thank goodness his neighbor was still home, and he didn't have to worry about running into her. Lacy didn't open her salon until nine o'clock, so he'd avoid his neighbor going early. Her name was Izzy, he couldn't keep calling her his neighbor. He had to start thinking about meeting her on the road all the time now when they were coming or going. The thought disturbed him. Why? She was a lady, and he had been around them before, so why was she different?

He pulled into the parking space and saw App and Stanley in the window as he headed inside.

He headed to the table beside App and Stanley, glad there was hardly anyone else in here at this early hour.

Sam grabbed a mug and a pot of coffee, grinning. "Good mornin', cowboy. I figured you'd be in early this mornin'. You've got questions, don't you?"

The two old checker players grinned as they watched and waited while Sam poured him a cup of coffee.

He stared at them all. "So, I came in for lunch yesterday and felt like I got set up by the matchmakers and you three helped."

Applegate hitched a bushy brow. "Well, *yeah*, that's what we're here for—entertainment. We said when you first arrived in town that you were goin' to be up for it. We just didn't know with who. But now we know. I'm gonna tell you when we heard Lacy had rented that house out, we had a feelin' you were a target. Don't look so shocked, it's because right now out there, it's just you and Izzy on that road. Sheri and Pace are in Australia. Kinda like when Pace and Sheri were the only two back when he first came to town. Anyway, I'm not saying y'all are a match, but it's fun to watch."

He had never heard App talk so much.

Stanley grinned. "Like my buddy said, it is fun to watch everyone try to sidestep the matchmakin' trio. Well, Lacy makes four, but she stands out on her own. If Lacy has her eye on you, then you're standin' on shaky ground. That is what you came to find out, right?"

"Yes, that's what I came to ask because I'm not here looking for..." He paused, he wasn't going to say love. "Anything other than helping out my friend while he's gone. Then I'll be looking for my own place, but if this keeps up, it won't be here."

Sam set his pot on the table beside the full coffee cup. "Look, cowboy, when you came to our town, ya knew it was famous. *And* ya knew what it was famous *for*. Everybody knows about Lacy Brown Matlock, Norma Sue Jenkins, Esther Mae Wilcox, and my sweet wife, Adela Ledbetter Green. Now, I can't defend them, other than to say they've made a huge number of great matches. Plus, it gives those ladies something to do. Fact is, they and their antics saved this dying town, and they really enjoy it. Get a kick out of it. In all honesty, if my Adela gets involved—well, I have to say God speaks through that lady, so you better watch out. I'm just letting you know you better be prepared. There is no tellin' what's comin'." He grinned, turned and walked to the cowboys who'd just walked in.

Luc watched the tiny, bowlegged cowboy businessman lead the other men to the far side of the diner. The man's words hung in the air. Yes, he'd known what this town was about, but in his mind, he figured it wouldn't touch him.

He'd been wrong. He turned his gaze and locked on the two checker players who were watching him with grins.

Applegate's normal grouchy look was a grin. It was odd to see—though he'd heard from many that over the years that grumpy look had evolved into a few more grins. He'd heard these two enjoyed getting involved, and now, looking at them, he knew…yep, he could be in trouble.

"You just got it, didn't ya?" Stanley asked as he looked from him to his checkerboard. He picked up his checker and hopped over one—two of Applegate's checkers.

App heard the double thump of the jump and yanked his gaze from Luc to the board. "Look there, I was thinkin' about what was going on with you and not paying attention," he growled. "I'm gonna get you back," he snapped, then looked at Luc. "Yeah, this is what happens when you lose track of where you're at or what's going on. You might make the wrong move or miss the signs. *Or* you might make the right move. We've seen cowboys like you do it all the time. So, I'm just warnin' you. Now, come play checkers. I'm done warning you. It's time to enjoy some checkers and relieve the stress that's got your face all scrunched up."

"He's right," Stanley agreed. "You're so scrunched up, you're looking like App there."

App gave his buddy a glare. "You'd be this wrinkled too if you didn't have those chubby cheeks. Now, forget all that hogwash, and let's play checkers. That's why we come to Sam's Diner. Believe me, it ain't to hear "Great Balls of Fire" for the six thousandth time. Or Elvis and his "Blue Suede Shoes." Those tunes are embedded into our minds forever. Thank goodness we can both turn our hearing aids down low if it gets too bad. But *you*, well, you at the moment can't turn anything down. The posse has you in there and you're about to be "All Shook Up."

It had been a wild and crazy first day. Thankfully she'd sat out on the porch on this second morning and had not walked up the hill through the rattlesnake-infested bluebonnets or jogged down the road for fear of seeing the good-looking-never-leave-her-mind Luc.

She drank her coffee feeling a little calmer. It was, after all, *she* who made the decisions about her life. She'd made the decision to be involved in the pig rodeo event for her grams. Just like she'd been the one who chose to come here and live out some fun times for them.

She'd prayed about it and felt confident that God understood and wasn't going to have her do anything that she didn't want to do. *Why?* Because *He* knew she was trying to fulfill her grams' dreams.

Now, this morning as she walked out of the house at eight-fifteen, she was heading to the salon a bit early. Lacy said she usually got there at a quarter to nine. Lacy had given her a key and told her to go in anytime she wanted to. So, if Izzy planned on getting there a little early, she'd have some alone time to get used to the place.

She was going in.

She climbed into her red Trailblazer, backed out of the driveway and headed down the curving dirt road. It was a pretty road with huge oak trees and pastures running along both sides. Honeysuckle vines grew along some of the fences along with wildflowers, including some bluebonnets—just not as many as behind her house.

She watched the beauty and also watched in her rearview hoping her neighbor wasn't driving to or from his house at the end of the road. She was going to have to get to jogging, and this was a great place to jog, and him being on this road made it seem a bit safer. The reality was she was going to have to get used to the fact that they were neighbors, and she was lucky he was a nice guy.

Lucky. She would think on the positive side of things. This morning the road was vacant and just hers, and she let her left arm hang out the window and felt the breeze on her skin, and smiled. *This is nice,* she thought as she rounded a corner—*holy cow!*

A gigantic Brahman bull stood in the middle of the road.

She yanked the wheel and headed for the ditch— bounced down it, out of it, then slammed through the barbed-wired fence and into one of the *huge* oak trees just on the other side...

Her airbag burst open, and her face slammed into it.

Dazed, she lifted her head. Everything spun, then she felt a really damp wetness against her cheek and turned her head toward the window and screamed. The gigantic bull had rammed its nose through her open window and licked her on the side of her face with his huge tongue!

In that instant, her brain shut down and she went blank again.

CHAPTER SEVEN

Luc was heading home from the diner, his mind still rolling with what had been said, when he saw the red SUV slammed up against the oak tree.

He slammed on his brakes, "*No.*" He threw the truck into park, shoved the door open then sprang into a run to help Izzy.

Mammoth stood next to the driver's window, his nose stuck inside. Now the bull was staring at him.

Luc shoved him aside. "Get *outta* the way," he growled, knowing instantly what had happened. He looked into the SUV and saw Izzy slumped in the seat and an airbag stuck in between her and the steering wheel.

He yanked the door open, the bull snorted, drawing

a shove from Luc's left hand. Mammoth better back away or he would find out which of them was the toughest. When the bull stepped back, Luc turned back to Izzy. Her forehead was bleeding a little, not much. It wasn't spitting blood out like a sprinkler, so that was great.

He leaned his knee on the door frame as he placed his fingers on her wrist—thank God she had a steady pulse.

"Izzy, come on, wake up. I'm so sorry Mammoth got out again. He's ornery and inquisitive, but despite me being furious at him, I know he didn't mean to do this. Come on, give me a look at those beautiful blue eyes of yours." His heart thundered as he shifted closer and gently cupped her face with his palm, willing those eyes to open. He prayed she would wake up and not be in any pain and that the cut on her forehead wasn't bad.

As he held her cheek, those eyes opened, and that blue sapphire sprang out like stars on a dreary day.

Those eyes had looked at him intensely in the diner yesterday and now, they slowly opened. His heart thundered as they fluttered open then closed again—

then she blinked and sat up like she'd been struck by lightning.

He backed up, giving her room but still holding her cheek.

"What happened?" she gasped. "*Oh*, the bull. Out again."

"Yes," he admitted softly. Now holding her arm with his free hand in case she passed out again. "It won't happen again. That bull is about to get penned up in an arena, with no escape, and then, if he doesn't get into behaving, he'll be gone. How do you feel?"

She inhaled slowly, her eyes clear now, sparkling—dazzling as they lifted up and looked at him once more. "I'm good." Suddenly a drop of blood dripped from the cut and dropped from her brow to her cheek. She saw it.

"I'm bleeding."

"Yeah, hang on." He needed to stop it since it was about to start dripping more now that it reached her brow and the only other place was to drip from there to her cheek. He had no handkerchief, so he yanked his T-shirt off over his head, wadded it up, then placed it on her forehead. "Sorry if it hurts," he said when she flinched.

"It's okay. Thanks. Is the bull okay?"

She had a cut forehead, and he was blotting the blood so it wouldn't get in her eyes, and yet she was wondering if the bull was okay. "He's ornery but fine. Now," he said gently. "Lean your head back a little and let's hold this in place for a few minutes."

She did as he asked, her hand automatically coming to take the cloth, their hands brushed, and his reaction was strong and mighty as he went on alert.

Whoa—she was beautiful, no denying it, but in that moment, he realized he was completely caught in the moment and needed to get his own head back on straight.

"Are you dizzy," he asked, getting back on track.

"No," she said, her eyes opening again, clearer. "Just thankful I listened to my gram and grammy. They're in heaven singing right now."

Maybe her head was worse than he thought. She was hearing her grammies singing. "Singing. Do you hear them singing often?" he asked, maybe she was hallucinating.

"Oh, *yes*, I hear them often," she said softly. "They sing to me when they're happy. My gram lived to be a hundred and six almost seven—she was about to sing to me one last time but closed her eyes and entered heaven. My grammy, her sweet daughter, lived to be eighty-seven and I loved every moment I had with them." She was talking softly and as if she were dreaming, she might have a concussion. "My mom didn't live as long as them, she died early, but I got to spend three years with her and Daddy."

"I'm sorry you lost them so early, but I'm glad you had your grandmothers. Are you sure your head isn't hurting really bad?"

She slid those eyes at him, and they twinkled. "Just a little thump. You know I'm here to work for Lacy, I gave up my hair styling business to take care of my grandmothers." She was talking faster now, but not rambling, the words were just flowing.

"Sounds like a great thing you did for them."

"I loved them. And was grateful for them, so it was what I wanted to do." Her eyes teared up and his heart cinched up.

"I'm sorry. I bet it was wonderful knowing your grams for so long but hard losing them."

She nodded. "Yes, of course I will never forget them, and I'm thankful."

"I understand. So, do you think you can get out?"

He pulled the shirt from her forehead and saw she wasn't bleeding any longer. Just a dribble, thank goodness. "Looks good so let's try."

He stood up, gently touched her knee as she moved it from the floorboard to the ground. He was thankful it wasn't caved in. She'd hit more on the passenger side, and he saw an indention over there. Her gaze went to the metal barb of the fence that was bent from her vehicle and then to the tree that had stopped her but thankfully not killed her.

Her troubled gaze met his and his stomach rumbled with a low roar that filled him—a roar of gratefulness that she was able to look up at him. That he was here for her.

Not wanting to go into how bad this could have been, he smiled encouragingly, needing to take her mind off of what could have been. "Okay, so let's do this. I'm going to take your elbows; you hang on to my forearms and let's make sure you can stand. Make sure nothing was hurt in that ride."

She placed her hands on his forearms, the heat that raged through him instantly took him by surprise. *What—*

"My grams are singing right now," she said, her words sounding like a song.

He almost chuckled, wondering what her grams would be singing to her but glad her words gave him a distraction from what was going on in his insides right now. "It sounds like they must have loved to sing."

"Yes, they did." Her eyes were on his as he helped her stand and then they dropped to his chest—his bare chest, and he saw a flash, then a small gasp. "Your shirt."

He'd frozen like she had. "Hang on." He looked down at her arms as he spoke, breaking the look they'd had. "I'll get you to step with me. Then I'll put that shirt back on."

Needing to be sure she could step out, he slid his right arm gently around her waist and held her as she took the first step.

"Okay, I'm not swaying, so that's a good thing."

"It's a great thing. Let's get you to my truck then we'll go back to your house and look over that cut—"

"*No*," she exclaimed sounding more focused. "There's no blood on my body except what's on your shirt now. So, Mr. Shirtless, you get me to your truck, then you can pull that T-shirt back on—if you want to. Thank goodness it's just a spot on it. Thank goodness it's not covered. *Then,* you can take me to Mule Hollow. *It's the place I'm supposed to be.*"

He was struck by her words. She sang them, and the tune was from something, but he couldn't remember where he'd heard it. The tune that played in his head—where had he heard that?

"*Heavenly Inspirations is the place I'm supposed to be.*"

It was there again, just a flow of the words, no singing this time but for some reason, he heard the tune again. Her gaze dropped to his chest, stuck there, then fluttered up and then over his shoulder. Only then did he remember he was naked from his jeans up and she knew it.

He worked sometimes in the sunlight with his shirt off and thought nothing about it. But standing here with a woman he barely knew had him feeling a little odd. Then again, thank goodness he'd been able to take it off or that little bit of blood would be dripping off her chin right now. And onto *her* shirt.

"Are you sure you want to go to the salon?"

"Yes, I am. I make it a point to not be late. And I'm certain Lacy has a lot of Band-Aids and alcohol to treat it with. In the hair-cutting industry, there is a need for Band-Aids. Sometimes, you accidently snip your fingers—the ones holding the hair up so the scissors can slice through the thin strip of hair easily. But accidents do happen and a bandage is needed. Those scissors we use are as sharp as swords, so yes, I know how to use a Band-Aid and not be late for work. I'm sure that Lacy can bring me back at the end of the day."

He nodded his head and sighed. "Okay, then, here we go." He held her with his arm around her waist as they walked up the slight incline to his truck. Mammoth stood to the side, but thankfully didn't join them.

He glanced at her and found her smiling. "It's a good thing to see that smile," he said. And it was a great smile. He stood there in the doorway as she turned, and he gently helped her get into the seat. He instantly missed the feel of her—what was he thinking?

His brain went back to that smile, man, he liked that smile and her dancing eyes. "What are you thinking about? You don't look like someone who could have just been hurt really bad or killed in an accident just now."

She sighed. "Well, you probably don't want to know…and I assure you it means nothing, but when things happen, well, okay. I'm here in Mule Hollow because both of my grandmothers were huge fans of Molly Popp's newspaper column. They hoped—okay, do not take this wrong—because I am *not* here to fulfill their dream for me to find a cowboy. I'm here to fulfill their *want to come to Mule Hollow for a visit*—that's it."

He was stunned by the firmness in her words and curious why she declared it so strongly. The question came out before he could stop it, "Why?"

She looked hesitant again. "Their wishful thinking and love of Mule Hollow and all it represented to them brought me here. But they'd both also been raised on *Green Acres*. Do you remember that old show? It originally aired a long time ago but still plays on some stations even to this day. My grams watched it until each of their lives ended, read their Bibles and Molly Popp's articles on Mule Hollow. Those were their loves. And me. I'm very grateful I had them."

His brain spun as he heard something in the back of his mind from his past as it slammed into him.

"Anyway, we watched reruns of *Green Acres*, and they wanted me to move here, check out Mule Hollow and fall in love. I *guarantee* you that is *not* why I'm here. I'm just here to fulfill the dream of *theirs* to visit for a short time. They get to watch me live out part of their dream while I figure out where I want to be since I don't have them to take care of anymore."

"So, what does *Green Acres* have to do with this good reason you've come to our small town?" he had to ask.

She blushed. *Whoa. Amazing. Why had that made*

her react that way?

"Well, see, my brain keeps going to them singing. All the way to town and since I arrived they've been singing their favorite song."

"And that's…" He wasn't getting it but wanted to.

"I was driving here and since I've arrived, I keep hearing them singing to me. They loved singing to me. Gram even had her sweet, small hairy dog that sat in her lap and added his odd tune to hers, like a backup singer."

He couldn't help it as the picture she'd brought into his head was precious…what special memories… He shoved *his* memories away not needing to go there but feeling terrible about how hard he'd shoved them. Never had he done that before.

He knew just how wonderful memories like hers could be—how much he'd always wanted more memories like that. But there was something in her eyes that looked as if she wasn't so sure at the moment.

"What?" he asked. "You don't seem enthusiastic about what you're thinking. Yet it sounds like a great memory."

She hitched her brows up. "It is. But see if you get

this: *Mule Hollow is the place to be...*" She sang the words in a soft, pretty tune. "*Heavenly Inspirations is where I'm meant to be. If I go there, I might get to meet the man—meet the man of my dreams—*

"*Meet the man of—*

"*my dreams.*

"*Meet the man of my dreams—*

"*Meet the man of—Meet the man of my dreams—*"

He was stunned by her tone, her musical magic and the tune—

"*Green Acres.*" He chuckled. Now getting it *big time*.

"Yes. Right on target. If you've ever listened to the intro to *Green Acres*, you'll hear the tune, not the words I just sang. Just the tune. And not exactly the same tune. Grams and Grammy got creative."

He busted out laughing as suddenly it all slammed into him. As the words she sang and the tune to the intro of the show *Green Acres* played in his head. He loved it. And that was the thought that he'd gotten earlier. He remembered his early days as he sat with his grandpa, who he'd lost early in his life. Grandpa had sat there beside him and they'd watched that famous old show together.

"Something good hit you just now?" she asked, her eyes gentle.

"Your grams could have been friends with my grandpa because I always watched that show with him before I lost him. Now I have those words playing in my brain." He smiled, and meant it.

She laughed at his words, and they both stared at each other and their laughter grew. He finally held up his hand trying to halt not only the laughter but the engaging feeling it sent through him as he watched her. The connection he suddenly felt—something he'd never felt before.

Something he *didn't want to feel*. Ever.

"Okay, I'm in agreement that those words and that tune are going to be playing through my head now for who knows how long." *And that look on your face as you sang them will also play before me.* "I'm afraid I'll never get it out of my head. Hey, don't suddenly look so alarmed—I'm not here to find love either. I'm just here to help out my horse trainer friend. I'm not looking for what the matchmakers are known for—*ever*."

Her eyes turned serious, but her softened smile was still there as her hand went to her heart. He wondered if her heart was pounding as hard as his was.

Get your thoughts straight and not on her face, those eyes or that song.

"Okay," she said. "We're in agreement. I'm here to give my grams a good time just for a few months. To let my grams enjoy it through me. Then I'll figure out where I want to reopen my salon. Where my business can grow and my life can start fresh in a larger city, not here in Mule Hollow with the man they *hope* I'll meet. So, what did you do before you came here?"

He reached over her and grabbed the seat belt, tugged it across her and plugged it into its holder. "I'm buckling you in, got to be sure you stay safe. These dirt roads, as you just found out, need seat belts plugged in also. You never know what's going to jump out in front of you, like you just learned. But I can promise you that it won't be Mammoth again." She was staring at him, the question still in her eyes. "I've spent the last several years out on huge ranches in Idaho. In the winters, you hole up with just your boots, heavy clothes, food, medicine, and medical kits to watch over the herd that you're assigned to. It's a quiet life of solitude in the hard winter months."

"Wow, you were like Pace Gentry."

"I'm here because of Pace. You know about him?"

"My grams read all the articles. Yes, the cowboy who lived like you did then got saved and was led to leave aloneness and be among people. And he came to Mule Hollow."

He smiled. "Yep, all true. Molly Popp never tells all of the stories, but she does make them entertaining."

"Yes, she does. There is always more to the stories, isn't there? You had a hard time that sent you into hiding like that."

He nodded, feeling a twist inside of him that he didn't want to feel. "I've been here almost a year now, and I came after Pace kept asking me to come help him out. That cowboy never gave up and the last time he asked I ended up saying yes. So, here I am."

CHAPTER EIGHT

Why had she told him about her grams' song? She must have really hit her head hard because her brain wasn't working right now. This cowboy—this unbelievably handsome, dark-headed cowboy had her attention whether she wanted to give it to him or not. Just the look in his *eyes* when he'd asked her how she was, had driven her heart into a rampage and she wasn't sure exactly what was going on.

And her grams' song played over and over—aggravatingly over and over in her brain. She was not from Mule Hollow. She was not wanting Mule Hollow to be in the song, and she did not want Luc to headline the song—tempting her heart. No, it was a no-no and where she didn't want to go.

Head raging, heart pounding inside the truck where she was stuck at the moment with the man on her mind. The good Lord needed to do some work because she'd come here for her grams, not for the craziness going on inside of her. The music played on and on…the tune of the old show rang on and her brain sang along—*Luc Asher is the man for you!*

He's handsome and a nice man too…

Hang on to him and you will see…

There's no other place you'd like to be—but in his arms forever… Stop!

She did not want Luc headlining the song in her brain…tempting her heart. No, that was a no—she wasn't going there. She needed to get her mind where it needed to be. Not on Luc. She'd come here because of her grams, to live for a few months for them the dream that had made them smile—to the song tune they also loved to sing in their last days on earth.

And now she was going nuts over the craziness going on inside of her.

Town came into view—*thank the good Lord.* "It is a great view from this far out," she said, grabbing onto the colorful town on the horizon.

82

His hand was gripping the steering wheel and her gaze dropped to his other hand gripping his thigh. His expression was serious, his gaze on the town did not shift to her.

Thank goodness. He didn't look pleased with what happened in their conversation. Yes, when she let the song loose, she had probably gotten it to play over and over in his brain too.

Whether she wanted it to or not, the tune and words were stuck in hers. "The colors jump out at you," she blurted out, needing something to change the subject in her brain.

He looked at her. "That's why Lacy had the townsfolks paint it those colors. It's supposed to jump out at you and call to you too. She got the idea after driving from Houston to Dallas and seeing the Sam Houston monument outside of Huntsville. When the statue was created and the highway was still just a four-lane, you could see that tall white statue from nine miles away for years. They say Lacy Brown had a vision to paint the dilapidated town, the dying gray and rusty town, give it a new life with paint. And that two-story pink salon and her famous pink caddy entering town was the dawning of a new town. And yep, that colorful town, like a ray of sunshine, has indeed, from all I've heard, brought people to Mule Hollow."

She smiled, she couldn't help it, the man was clearly irritated by the idea. His words didn't show it, but his expression did. His tense jaw and the fact that his eyes were now glued to the town and not darting back to her. She totally understood. She knew the story, knew all of it well. Her gram and grammy made sure of it. She knew most people in Texas or other states had traveled the road I-45 between the big cities Houston and Dallas and had seen the tall white statue. And yes, as a child she'd first seen it. Now the highway which was the escape route for the coastal towns to escape hurricanes had been widened and the view was shorter, but she remembered being a little girl and asking Grammy, "What is that?"

"You'll see, sweet girl. We'll stop and look at it. But just watch it because it's Sam Houston, and he's going to get bigger and bigger with every mile we drive."

And he did. And now, the colorful town was doing the same. Just like Lacy had envisioned it. "I have to say, until you arrive and see the colorful town on the landscape, you don't really get just how it stands out. I mean, I knew—had been told just how colorful it was, pink, blue, purple, red, yellow. It's amazing. And like usual I can see my grams' excitement." She didn't say most of the excitement was from the fact that she was in the truck alone with this handsome cowboy who had rescued her in her time of need.

It didn't matter that the bull that had caused her wreck was his bull. They were probably happy because that bull, in their mind, was kind of kin in spirit to Samantha the donkey—the matchmaking donkey that had helped bring many together. She had to meet the mischievous burro for them but also because she loved the stories of Samantha, the banana-LaffyTaffy-eating donkey, and the laughter they brought to her grams.

And that joy was a big part of why she was here— and as her glance shifted to Luc, she reminded herself of that.

She was here for her grams, not to fall in love.

Luc pulled up in front of Heavenly Inspirations, glad to see it. Then again not glad to see it. Everyone in town was going to know that his untamed bull had done this to Izzy. He spotted Lacy's pink caddy sitting in front of the building. Sometimes she drove her caddy and sometimes she drove her red SUV. Clint had told him with their two little boys, he'd asked her to drive something easier to get the kids around in, and she'd gladly agreed. But she still drove her caddy a lot.

His brain went back to the lady sitting in the passenger's seat. What would work best? Ah, all kinds of information and what would work best since the other vehicles told him that the salon was going to be packed. Esther Mae, Norma Sue, and Adela were there waiting along with a lot of others, the cars told him so…but one look to the salon window and he knew it for certain. Everybody was packed inside that salon waiting to welcome Izzy Cranberry to town.

And after they found out what happened, he was never going to hear the end of it…

Izzy pushed open her door as soon as he put the truck in park, but he acted on full speed, rammed the gearshift into park and sprang from the truck. He rounded the passenger's side of the truck before she put her feet on the pavement. Thankfully he reached her before she eased from the truck.

Obviously, someone spotted them because in the blink of an eye a herd came busting out the salon door. Norma Sue Jenkins stood out in her ruby red overalls, Esther Mae in her spicy yellow knee britches, speckled flip-flops topped off with her flashy rainbow-toned blouse. Behind her stood Adela, her sapphire observant eyes glowing along with her gentle smile, and behind her stood Lacy, backed by a huge group of ladies.

He placed his hand on her lower back and took her elbow into his other hand and helped her to the ground from the high seat of the truck, making sure she could walk.

"Walk carefully," he urged, feeling sparks shooting up his arm from touching her.

"I can do this on my own," she said only to him.

In reply, he tightened his grip on her elbow, but still being gentle. "I'm not letting you go," he whispered. "We'll walk up the steps and into the salon. And then

I'll let the ladies take care of you."

"*Let us take care of her*—what happened?" Norma Sue demanded as her gaze hit on Izzy's blood-crusted forehead

Esther Mae's did too. "Oh, my word! She has a forehead cut. What happened?"

In that instant, everyone saw Izzy's injury and whether he was going to keep his hold on her or not was no longer up to him. He was instantly booted out of the way by Norma Sue, who grabbed Izzy's arm from him, and Esther Mae reached her other side and slid her arm around the back of Izzy's waist. Secure and careful they walked toward the salon as the other women parted to let them pass.

And Luc was forgotten, plain and simple.

CHAPTER NINE

"I'm okay," Izzy declared, her voice shaky.

"Well, you don't look it," Lacy exclaimed, holding the door open as the group separated and left a trail for Norma Sue and Esther Mae to get her inside.

At least Luc no longer had a hold on her and that was a relief—then why did it feel like she'd just lost? Needing a distraction, she looked around the beauty salon. "I love it." And she did.

"We're glad you do. But right now, sit down in this salon chair, and I'm going to look at this cut. Luc, what happened to her?"

At the call, Izzy glanced across the room to where he stood just inside the front door surrounded by women of all ages.

He looked uncomfortable and that sent a regret through her.

"It's my fault, ladies," he said. "My bull escaped the fence on our dirt road and Izzy was coming to work early on her first day. The bull startled her as she came around the curve and she ended up swerving, went through a ditch and a fence, and was stopped hard by an oak tree. Thankfully I came upon her right after it happened. She woke up and wouldn't let me take her to a hospital. She wanted to come here to be on time for her first day at Heavenly Inspirations. So, I'm just going to say that I'm praying that Heavenly Inspiration comes down and intervenes here. I say again, I'm so sorry the bull got out and I can tell you," he said, yanking his hat off his head, "with sincere regret, I'm really sorry, Izzy. But I know this is where you want to be, so I'm going to back out now and go take care of that bull. He won't be endangering anyone again. Ladies, take care of her."

With that, he spun on his heel, strode out the door and, though her eyes watched him leave, she lost him as he rounded the brick wall that blocked his truck from her view.

Instantly everyone started throwing questions at her. And she yanked her gaze from the now empty space and stared down at her trembling hands. *Why?*

Her eyes were a little blurry—from what? *Tears?*

Oh, no, she blinked hard then looked up. Determined that no one read anything into this other than an outrageous morning.

"I dodged a bull, and it got me in trouble, but here I am." She smiled big—huge. "I'm sorry that on my first day I needed someone to put a Band-Aid on my forehead. But we get that done, then I'll get up and we'll start—if anyone trusts my hands on their hair."

Hands went up and so her first day styling hair at Heavenly Inspirations began. And it was a great day.

A fun day.

She hadn't been sure of that at the beginning of the day, but miraculously it had become a wonderful, great day. Even if she did have a bandage on her forehead. She liked it here. Everyone was so welcoming.

At five o'clock their last customer left the salon and Izzy turned and smiled at Lacy. "Thanks, I loved today."

"So did I." Lacy sat down in her salon chair crossed

91

her legs and drummed her long pink fingernails on the arm of the chair. "Now that we're alone let's talk about it."

Izzy sat in the chair that was now hers. "Are you going to tell me I'm already fired?"

Lacy threw her head back and laughed. "Oh, no, I'm not. You know you're doing great. Everyone is crazy about you. I just had that feeling when you called looking for a job. But, what we're talking about right now is you don't have a vehicle. You had to have it towed in?"

"Yes, I did. I was going to ask you if you could give me a ride home. I'm not sure if there is a rental company anywhere near, but I could find one and have a car delivered tomorrow. I should have already called, but I was having so much fun meeting everyone, I didn't. It was a really great day."

Lacy waved her hand. "No, no, no. You do not have to rent a car. I'm going to tell you Clint is coming to meet me at the diner with the boys, and he can take me home. There he is pulling in at Sam's Diner. You can come have an early supper with us. Clint picked them up from the daycare for me. Or if you need to go ahead and leave, you'll take my caddy. It's a great caddy and your grams will be happy looking down watching you cruise around in it—"

"Oh, no, I can't do that. You love that car."

"Yes, you can. Besides you're here fulfilling the dream of your grandmas. I can tell you if they read about Mule Hollow, they read a lot about my pink caddy. It's been through a lot of good times and is so fun to ride in. Me and that caddy rescued Molly from a raging bull, and I drove the roads and found cattle rustlers in it and so much more. Believe me, that caddy has been through a lot and helped a lot of…unsuspecting people find their way. So, you're going to drive it now as long as you need it. But right now, since I'm done for the day, I'm heading over to the diner for an early supper with my fellas then heading home. You can take the caddy; you might even take it on a long drive at night. If your grams read Molly's articles, then they knew that I'm a restless person and drive my caddy late at night. Not so much now, but in the early days I did."

"They told me you did. Why not now?"

Lacy's head tilted and her blue eyes sparkled with delight. "I sleep better now because my boys wear me out before I put them to bed, and then my sweet Clint is holding me tight." She chuckled. "And I love every moment of my life. But you, my single friend, should try the night drive because the wind in your hair, the stars glistening from above, it's like a sweet lullaby coming from a sparkly sky bringing joy and peace from the Lord for any kind of problem—not that I'm saying you're having problems, it's just a wonderful way to spend an evening."

Her head was spinning at Lacy's words, like the woman was digging deep without realizing she was—or did she know what she was doing?

"So," Lacy continued. "You take it with my blessing and you're going to have a good time—unless that handsome cowboy who just pulled up is coming to offer you a ride and you'd rather do that."

Cowboy. Her gaze shot to the window and there, getting out of his truck, was Luc. Startled, she gasped, "He's not coming to pick me up. We didn't plan that."

"I have a feeling he realized he didn't offer you a

ride home, so he's come to ask."

"I don't need him, I have your car—thank you very much," she said, the words rushing.

Lacy chuckled as if not believing her and stood up as the door opened, and whether she wanted to admit it or not, she was happy when that good-looking cowboy stuck his head inside.

And if that wasn't enough, he swept his hat from his head and that dark wavy hair was now visible as his gaze locked on to her. "I came to offer you a ride home since I didn't offer it this morning."

"Take it easy, girl," Lacy was standing there grinning. Looking from him to her.

She fought not to stumble on her words, "Thank you, but Lacy is lending me her pink caddy for a few days."

"Really, you're going to drive the caddy?"

She stuck her fist to her hip. "Yes, is there a problem with that? Or do you think I'm going to run into another bull, hog or some other animal?"

"No, I was just thinking about you driving the pink Cadillac. I got the bull put up, so he won't be a problem.

And as weird as it sounds, he's not a bad bull. He's just standing in the arena looking like a big dog waiting to be petted."

"A *very* big dog," Izzy responded, and unable to stop herself, she laughed, and so did Lacy, but Luc was staring at her.

"Why don't you join us at the diner, Luc," Lacy suggested. "Clint and our boys will be at Sam's too."

Izzy almost gasped. Surely he would say no.

Luc just stood there with his hands clutching his Stetson. He wanted to stay because he was an idiot—but he knew he was going because they'd invited him, and Izzy was going too. This might be a better way to be around her with Clint and Lacy and those cute little boys. And in the diner, everyone would see him and Izzy with Lacy and Clint and words might start churning. But after they reached the diner, he hurried to open the door.

A squeal went up as Lacy entered and her young son came running at her from the table where he'd been standing beside his dad. "Mama!" he yelped as his mom swept him into her arms and spun them around. Between Lacy's light hair and his fluffy white hair, they looked like Cool Whip whirling around.

She halted after a moment, bent over and gave her smiling cowboy a kiss and in that moment, Luc's insides yanked to alert—what would it be like to be loved like that? His gaze shot to Izzy—why, he wasn't sure, but her gaze was locked on the happy couple too. She had an amazed look on her beautiful face, and then her gaze came to his and they just stood there.

Her eyes dug deep—he'd never looked at a woman whose eyes captivated him—or decapitated him. He wasn't sure in that moment which was the right description because he had no brains. All he knew was this beauty was looking at him and he couldn't look away. Then, she blinked and yanked her gaze away to watch Lacy pick up her baby from his high chair and cuddle him.

He met Clint's watching eyes and his friend smiled. "Hey, buddy, glad you came on over. We have plenty of room. With you and Miss Izzy here, we might draw a crowd."

Ignoring the comment, he grabbed the small table

and set it so the tops connected, then grabbed the chairs and placed one on his side and one on the other side.

"Looks good," Sam said, as he ambled up. The little man held out his hand for a handshake like no other.

Luc had learned to brace himself because this little dude had a grip like nothing he'd ever experienced before. He lifted his hand and Sam took hold so firm it felt like he was in a cattle shoot about to get a needle plunged into his hip. He couldn't move as Sam grinned up at him while squeezing and shaking his hand vigorously.

"They tell me my grip is supposed to get easier as I age, so I'm practicing to keep it strong. What do you think?" Sam's grip tightened as he kept shaking.

"You've got one iron grip that's for sure." Luc caught Clint's grin. No telling how often this had happened to the long-time resident.

"Yup, How am I doin'?"

Luc grinned—rather than grimacing. "Great and you're looking younger every time you squeeze harder. Not that I want you to keep squeezing. The truth is, if you've been shaking like this all your life, no wonder your arms are so muscled up." Sam released Luc's hand,

and he stuffed it into his pocket so it could rest.

Sam's eyes glittered. "For a tiny man like me, I've always had a hard grip, made people know *not* to mess with me. Big men like you and Clint, people already know not to mess with y'all. You've got that serious look on your face right now, so I could be in trouble for messing with you."

Izzy crossed her arms and looked at the two of them as if trying to figure them out.

"What?" he asked, unable not to.

"You two sound like y'all challenge each other all the time."

Sam crossed his arms. Muscles bulging, he said, "I hope I challenge everybody. How about you? What challenges you, young lady? A big ole handsome cowboy like this one?"

The expression of shock on her face was worth a shout-out, but he kept his mouth shut.

However, Lacy did not, she waved her long nails in the air. "You got it, Sam. Isn't that right, girlfriend?"

Izzy looked like she wanted to throw up. "Sure, *real* funny. This cowboy and I just have a few—well, I'm not sure what we have." She couldn't look away from him as his lip hitched to the side.

"Yesterday, I rescued her from a rattlesnake, and I don't think she liked it too much. Which I find strange since I could have just let it strike her. *Then* this morning I gave her a ride to town after I rescued her from my crazy bull, that is now locked up and sad about it. So, I'm not sure what to do about it. Not sure if I have anything now to apologize for."

"You have nothing to apologize for," she said firmly.

"Okay then, I'll just warn you that you might want to watch out for these matchmakers." The words came out before he could stop them.

Her sapphire eyes darkened. "I've made it clear that I'm not looking for a match. I already said that, so I guess I'll just have to say this out loud so anyone and everyone in this room can hear them—I'm *not* looking to be matched up. I'm here to live the dream of my grams of living life in Mule Hollow and that's all." Then she sat down in the chair, crossed her arms and looked at Sam who was standing there clearly enjoying the show he'd started. "Mr. Sam, please bring me a cup of black coffee."

Sam grinned. "Yes, ma'am, I can. Anybody else want something?" His gaze locked on Luc.

"No, sir. Right now, I'm just fine. Not sure how long I'll be here. But I'll make it."

"You don't even want water?" Izzy asked like a challenge as their gazes locked over something stupid like water.

He saw the twinkles in the corners of those amazing eyes. She was messing with him. He took the challenge. "Sam, I'll take water, a *big* glass of water." He sat down in the chair across from Izzy, placed his hands on the table and locked his fingers together.

A sign he hoped said he wasn't going to be the one to look away. She could stare at him all she wanted, he just wasn't sure what she was challenging him for.

What he did know was, if he didn't watch out, he could stare at this lady for the rest of his life.

And be happy—and *that*, him being happy, was mind-boggling.

CHAPTER TEN

Why was she challenging him? And he knew she was. He was probably wondering the same question as they stared across the table at each other. Sam went away. She knew he'd bring her coffee, but his ambling walk had a little spring in it as if he was happy about something.

Lacy sat down beside her. "Whoa, you two are looking like y'all might want to go out to dance or a duel."

"We don't want to do either," Izzy said, trying to sound sensible despite not feeling that way at all. What was wrong with her?

"Then, a drive in my pink caddy will help that serious look on your face disappear. Take that neighbor of yours on a drive. A moonlight drive."

"Lacy, don't go there," the words came out before she could stop them.

Lacy hitched a brow. "I'm just sayin', a moonlight drive helps in a lot of ways."

Dumbfounded, Izzy stared at her new friend whose eyes were dancing. "You are *exactly* like my grams said you were."

Lacy beamed. "Yep, yep, yep! I have a feeling they got me."

Yes, they did. Here she was sitting in the diner exactly where her grams wanted her to be. They'd set her up before they died.

And Lacy Brown Matlock knew it. Oh dear Lord, what had she done? Her grams were watching from above, and this was not the show Izzy was willing to star in.

Sam broke the moment, thank goodness, as he set her cup of black coffee in front of her. "Here ya go." He winked at her then turned and started taking orders from everyone else. Thankfully giving her a moment to get her head back on straight.

Only then did she realize she'd been rude by demanding coffee. She'd been distracted by the cowboy sitting across from her. The cowboy who was now not saying anything.

Instead, his gaze, when she lifted her eyes to look at him was on the cute little boy sitting beside him. The little boy who was playing with the model horse. As she looked, he grinned up at Luc and Luc grinned at him. "That's a good-looking horse you have there."

"I'm learnin' to ride my real horse—fastest horse there ever was. My daddy, he's a good teacher, and he tells me that I know how to hang on tight, and I do. Do you?"

She got tickled by the little blond-headed fella's face as he stared up at the handsome cowboy. What a match they made.

Luc rubbed his jaw. "Well, I tame horses. They say I'm pretty good at it."

"Me too. I help Daddy out on the ranch a lot. We're going to go put some cows out...but only after the rodeo. I get to try and catch a muddy pig. I'm lookin' forward to it. Daddy and Mama told me they are little and greased so they're hard to catch and carry. I think you guys are going to chase a different one." He looked at Izzy. "Are you gonna catch one with the ladies?"

"They talked me into it."

"Us kids are getting to chase them too—or sheep. But the ladies love getting all dirty." He hooted. "I didn't get to do it last year, but I got to watch. They got so muddy and greasy, it was fun. I laughed a lot."

Izzy chuckled but could see she had signed up for an ordeal. She was going to be one greasy, dirty, pig-fighting gal come this weekend. She raised her hand and the little boy looked at her. "So, you're saying I'm going to be a nasty mess?"

His blue eyes sparkled like his mom's. "Yep, yep, but it'll be fun, and I'll watch you if you watch me."

"Can't pass that up," she said, her heart tugging.

He shook his head and grinned. "I'll show you how it's done."

She chuckled and met Luc's gaze. "I hear from the ladies that I'm supposed to help you get ready for that since I don't get to be involved."

"No need. I'd just as soon learn from the beginning

like everyone else. They all told me that training wasn't going to help me much."

He hitched a brow. "Okay, like I said I wasn't expecting this, but if you want to try, you know where to find me. I have some horses to break and a bull to tend to. So, enjoy your meal." He got up and walked away.

It had been a long, busy few days for Luc. He'd ridden his horses, thought about his neighbor—even when he didn't want to. He'd driven up the road past the house and avoided Sam's and the salon. He'd holed up at the house at night, sitting out on the back porch trying *not* to think about his neighbor. Tomorrow was the rodeo and there would be no avoiding seeing her.

Maybe he could avoid talking to her. That would be the ideal situation despite the fact that no matter how much he tried not to think about her, he did. Meaning tomorrow was going to be a hard day.

The moonlight was shining bright, and the stars were twinkling high up in the night sky. He tried not to think but his mind went to where he was out on the backside of a gigantic Idaho ranch. Then his mind would wander back to his life… The life that was hard to think about, hard to leave behind, and hard to move forward from.

Pace had told him he had to step forward, he had to leave behind the pain and remember the good times. He didn't have to forget the family he'd lost, but he couldn't let his past rule his future.

And as he sat there with his coffee—coffee that he shouldn't be drinking at eleven o'clock at night, but he couldn't resist it. Better to drink coffee than alcohol. There had been a time when he'd made the wrong choice of drink, a time when the only way to get away from his past was to drink so much his brain couldn't work right. But thank the good Lord, he'd overcome that and replaced it with coffee. Coffee didn't interfere with his sleep. There was too much other stuff that interfered with his sleep, so he couldn't blame it on coffee.

But right now, all he saw as he looked up at that sky, that beautiful bright moonlight and the twinkling stars, was the time when he'd let his lost dreams fill his heart and mind. When he had plans for his life. Plans for a wife and family that he would never have.

His aching heart had recovered somewhat, but unless you'd lived what he'd lived through, nobody could tell him that it would ever be fully gone. He knew Pace had told him that there were some cowboys in Mule Hollow who had been through really hard sorrow, and if he talked to them, it might help. But it was too personal, so he sat alone and stared up at the sky and tried to let this be enough.

But tonight, it wasn't.

Standing up, he didn't pick his coffee cup up as he strode through the moonlit yard toward what was the horse arena but held a bull right now. He reached the pen, and there stood Mammoth, the huge black bull. They eyed each other.

"How are you doin' tonight, big fella?"

The huge bull snorted and scratched his paw in the dirt, but instead of charging, he walked slowly toward Luc. Luc felt that need that he'd felt often and almost opened the gate, walked inside, and locked the gate behind him.

He wanted to anger the bull, to let it charge at him. But he didn't. He couldn't let the bull take his life no matter how hard he'd wanted to at first.

When he first went to Idaho to hide from everything, Pace had come into his life and told him that God would work in his life, change his life, he just had to let Him. Had to not think of his pain and put others first.

Put others first…

That ache, that throb in his gut in the back of his heart. That strain that wanted to get angry and rebel and tell God He could have saved his father, mother or his sister—but He didn't. Why?

He sighed, dropped his head to his arms that were stuffed through the metal railings and then rested his head on his biceps. Inside the pen, his hands were gripped together but he wasn't praying. Just trying to figure out why they'd all been taken in one horrible crash. God might know, but he never would know or understand.

He suddenly felt warm air on his hands and looked up, feeling moisture in his eyes, moisture he tried not to feel but couldn't defeat in some moments. As he lifted his gaze, he stared into the black eyes of Mammoth.

"I'm not as tough as I look either. So, here's the deal. I'm going to help you learn to calm down so you can get out there and be free again. I'm going to help you and maybe God's going to help me somehow feel free again. If I can let myself.

"I don't know, but if I need to be kicked in the gut, then go for it.

"But I'm going to make sure you don't do it to anyone else. If anyone deserves a kick from you, it'll be me. So, we're going to start working, but I have a rodeo tomorrow, so Sunday after church it'll be me and you, dude. Now, go enjoy your night and your day tomorrow, and thanks for giving me that glare."

He opened his hand and rubbed the bull's jaw. He was one tough cookie. Just like Luc had once thought he was. But life showed him he wasn't.

He knew now there was a power greater than him. A power that he didn't totally understand.

A power that had left him alive, and he didn't know why.

Why him?

That short time at that huge ranch, where they'd worked together, Pace had looked him in the eyes and told him what happened wasn't his choice. His family had died and he'd lived, he would never know the reason, but the outcome was of Luc's making.

Pace, the quiet recluse who had taken Jesus into his heart and finally realized he had to share his experience with others. So he had come out of hiding and he told Luc God had a plan for him too.

Luc hadn't believed him. How could God have a plan for him when he couldn't find his way out of the grief?

But finally, after one more call from Pace, Luc had come to Mule Hollow, loneliness had driven him to find a new way.

If God have a plan for him he was ready because hiding out alone and grieving wasn't the way he could pay tribute to his lost family.

And since coming to Mule Hollow, he'd been blending in for the most part, at least having more life than he'd known in years. Until tonight he'd thought

111

he'd found a new way of life. He hadn't had this hard a time in a while.

So why was tonight different? He turned and strode back toward the cabin and looked up at the stars.

Why was he here? And why, when he looked up in that sky, did he see the sparkling blue eyes of his new neighbor?

CHAPTER ELEVEN

"It's going to be a great night," Esther Mae grinned, rubbing her hands together.

Izzy tried not to panic. She'd had a rough last two days, knowing this was coming but having promised Tate, Lacy's little boy, that she'd do it, she would, and she was going to make him proud. If he remembered her and what he'd asked of her.

It must have hit him just a few minutes earlier when his daddy had let the little fella out to ride sheep and Tate made sure she was watching him. That was what he was doing, not wrestling a pig. Izzy was going to catch a pig, maybe wrestle it, probably roll in the mud since they'd wet the dirt down just for that—maybe she'd roll in cow poop. She wasn't sure what was going to happen. And that glow in Esther Mae's eyes didn't help.

"Aww, come on now, you know you're going to get out there and let that panic look in your eyes go away," Norma Sue said as she reached out and slapped her on the back—it was probably supposed to be a pat of encouragement, but it was more like a slap to get her ready. Well, she needed that alright because she was far from ready.

She looked at Norma Sue. "Thanks, Norma Sue. I wish I had the guts that you have, ranching woman. All day today at the salon, everyone talked about what a great cattlewoman you are. That you and your sweet husband Roy Don have worked this ranch since Lacy's father-in-law was alive. They said y'all were two fantastic rodeo competitors."

Norma Sue's smile spread wide across her chubby face and her curly gray head of hair leaned to one side as she clapped her hand to her heart. "Oh, yeah, honey. I lived for my rodeo days. I lived for catchin' me a cow and wrestling it to the ground and tying its feet together after I had jumped off a horse and flipped it over. Yep, you look at my belly now and wonder how in the world I did that. You might not can tell now, but I used to have some strong muscles. And my hubby, that man could rope, ride and fly off the back of a horse to win the competition of wrapping those hooves together. There was no better cowboy than that man of mine. But these days he does the announcing and does a great job entertaining. And then, no worries for you, there will be cowboys out there on the back of some fast horses to save you or protect you if you need it. If by chance you get attacked by a crazy little pig, you just don't worry, someone will save the day. I think you're going to do a great job though. Hold that arm up and let me see that muscle."

Izzy laughed, unable to help it as she lifted her skinny arm, tightened it so the small muscle she had bulged. "It's not big, but I do work it out. So maybe it'll do me some good."

"It's that grin I was really looking for. Stop being negative. Be positive and get out there and have a good time. Believe me that rodeoing is a great time. Some people love it for the competition but others, like me, just love it for the challenge and fun. There's nothing better than using your strength to accomplish something, flipping a cow or achieving a goal. The only thing better is me catchin' my hubby and planting a big kiss on his lips." She winked and grinned.

Everyone laughed, Esther Mae, Lacy, and even Adela standing off to the side taking it all in with that soft expression and those eyes that saw everything.

"Yep," Esther Mae added. "Life can be an adventure. All manner of adventures, but God made it so that we might endure troubles, but we could also have fun. So, you, sweet lady, have a good time. A Mule Hollow good time. And I think you're going to like the two cowboys who just entered the ring to watch out over all the piglet hunters."

She wasn't sure how to take it all in as the ladies tried to encourage her. Then Norma Sue, Esther Mae, and Adela turned and walked away, grinning as they headed toward the stands where they would watch the pig catching from midway up the bleachers. A great view, they'd told her, where they could see everything and root for her.

She couldn't see in the arena, so she looked at a grinning Lacy and Molly, who was there to write an article. Their eyes were glistening.

"What is so funny, and *why* did she say that? *Who* is out there?"

Molly tapped her finger on her crossed arms. "Well, let's just say I have an article to write after this, and I'm looking forward to whatever goes on out there. My readers love these rodeos, especially the pig wrestling because they never know what's going to happen. And who they were talking about, well, you'll see, just take a peek through the fence down toward the end. You just get out there and have a good time. My sweet little fellas are waiting on me with Stacy, who watches the kids while their parents are busy helping out. That Stacy is amazing. When they came here a few years ago in that van from California and that quiet Stacy climbed off that van so withdrawn, carrying that tiny baby of hers, none of us would have ever believed she'd be the best daycare keeper in all the world. She even brings her talent to the rodeos for us while we do our thing. Her equally quiet hubby watches over them all until he has to go help get the rodeo going. He's a great, quiet cowboy. God blessed us the day that group came here in that bus. I understand that you're interested in Rose, who also rode in on that van. Her and her sweet Max. Max is a great young man and all the young ladies have crushes on him. You'll see in a few moments. Okay, I'm taking us off of our subject, but I think you needed some distraction. I hear you went over and met Max and Rose at the Prickly Pear Jelly store."

"Yes, I did, and he is one good-looking young man focused on his business. My sweet grams read about him when he first got off that van that brought him and his mom and the other ladies and kids from California to Mule Hollow." She smiled thinking about her grandmothers. "They were hoping he found love but didn't last long enough to see it happen. But he is serious about his business. And his mom and that cowboy of hers go together so well. As they would say, a match made in heaven with a little help from the matchmakers of Mule Hollow." She grinned big at her words of memory. It was as if they were smiling down at her for her thoughts. "I've had prickly pear jelly on my toast for years that they special ordered from them."

"That's wonderful. Okay, I better get going. You do good out there." Molly smiled and headed off.

Lacy had let them talk and now she spoke up and focused on Izzy. "Molly loves her life here, and her articles are wonderful. Obviously, your grams enjoyed them. I like how they attached to Max. He's decided they're going to open stores all over Texas, and their first new store is going into a town called Dew Drop, Texas. They have so many big fans out there. The diner owner there of the Spotted Cow Café is a lover of her jelly and started ordering it and selling it in the diner to those who tried it and fell in love. It's a cattle town like Mule Hollow. They'll have it opened in a couple of months. Max is excited enough that he might be opening Prickly Pear Jam stores all over Texas."

"That would make my grams happy. They said he rides horses too."

"Yes, he does. He's become a cowboy like all the men in town. He's good, and he can rope with the best of them. Anyway, now that you're distracted and calmer, I'm going to follow Molly and let you get ready to wrestle—I mean catch a greased-up piglet." She grinned and her blue eyes danced. "You can do it but have fun." And then Lacy waved her long-fingernailed hand and strode away in the same direction Molly had headed to the stands.

And Izzy, she stood there once again facing the arena that would soon be full of running, romping, greased piglets—at least one of which she was expected to catch.

Oh, sweet Grams, if you ever happened to think I might not love you or do anything for you—well, this proves that I will.

Luc sat in the saddle of his horse that could move around in the cows like a ballerina it was so quick on its hooves. It was a bunch of ladies who had lost their minds. He glanced over at Max, and the young cowboy was grinning. The ten years difference in their ages was clear. This young cowboy was looking for a good time.

"So, you are going to save them if they need it?"

Max grinned over at him, his eyes glowing. "Sure I

am. You should see this fiasco. I've been watching it since I came here at sixteen. It's a hoot to watch. Those little pigs aren't going to hurt the ladies. Mostly they're going to cause them to fall into the mud, maybe one will jump on them in an effort of trying to escape being caught and squeezed from the ladies trying to hang onto their greasy little bodies."

He was chuckling as he spoke. "It's not like they're a big ole hog or an angry bull. They're little fat-bellied piglets. They weigh a little bit but not really anything. The mud is going to get them more than the pig, and yeah, we're going to have to go in and pull them out of the mud and sometimes from beneath a pig. So, don't be worrying. I know my job, have done it two years in a row and it's been fun."

"Fun." Luc wasn't so sure but Max seemed to enjoy it.

"Yeah, I'm not lookin' for love, but there are a few cute gals out there that will have their sights on me. And I've got to tell you, they ask me to dance, and I get out there and dance, but it doesn't mean I'm lookin' for love. Some of those gals are out there because they are just havin' fun like me and not lookin' for love. But most of them have eyes for a husband, and I'm tryin' to stay away from them. But they're going to do all kinds of crazy things to get my attention that's going to make my head spin out of saneness, and I'm going to fall in love and change all my plans." He laughed, his eyes dancing with humor.

"I can look at them right now, there are three for sure and they're going to roll around in the mud until I come to save them. So, yeah, if you see those three over on the side there. That small redhead and that poofy blonde-headed gal and the black-headed gal that are standing there close together in those colorful cowgirl boots and those glistening jeans, well, they're waiting on me. So, if you see them rolling around in the mud, don't go riding to their rescue because I will. You don't want to get them hooked on you because it's hard to get unhooked. They come to *everything* we hold."

"No kidding."

"Everything. *But,* those over there, in case you're lookin' for love, they're older than those I just pointed out, so the lucky woman may be out there, and I'll leave them to you."

Luc was floored. "I'm not interested. I just got asked by the ladies to help out."

Max laughed. "Those matchmakers picked you for a reason. Me too."

Holy moly—so that was why those three asked him to do this. They were trying to get him matched up. His brain was frying with sizzling heat that had nothing to do with attraction to anyone. He had fallen to their conniving again. But at least he hadn't had to help his neighbor try to catch a pig.

His gaze landed on Izzy in that instant, standing on the outskirts of everyone. She was trying hard to look like she wasn't nervous, but he knew one thing for sure—she wasn't wanting him to have to come rescue her. But whether he wanted to or she wanted him not to, if she needed him, he was riding in.

He'd be there for the rest of them too. Although, this was Mule Hollow so the twelve gals beside Izzy, planning to wrestle a greasy piglet or pig were probably hunting for more. Prospecting for a husband would probably fit better.

His brain spun at the idea. For relief he focused on the pigs. Which he hadn't seen yet and wasn't sure what size was coming out of that gate when it flew open.

Other than Izzy he was the only one wondering because those young ladies staring at good-looking Max were definitely not thinking about the pigs. The tall, lean cowboy had a look about him and those young gals were definitely here to gain Max's attention. But, there were more than the three or four Max knew were here with their eyes on the young cowboy.

Luc was just going to let the Max have fun while he watched out for everyone. His gaze went to Izzy— determined Izzy. He knew for certain no one was prettier than her. Or looking more determined.

He suddenly realized that if anyone out there was resolute to catch a greased-up pig or piglet, no matter what the size, it was Izzy. That woman had a stubborn stamina about her. If he jumped in to protect her she'd probably get riled up.

He wouldn't interfere unless needed. And he had a feeling, as his gaze scanned the other ladies it slammed into him, that he was being watched too.

There were at least four ladies, gazes locked onto him like hunters. This was going to be one wild and *crazy* night...no other way to describe it...and him, he was stuck.

CHAPTER TWELVE

The show was about to begin as Sheriff Brady walked out to the middle of the arena as if putting everyone on alert.

On the loudspeaker, Roy Don, Norma Sue's husband, called out, "Okay ladies, Sheriff Brady is going to give y'all a wave to get ready then he's going to go behind the railing so y'all can get the rodeo started. But, just wanted to say if you need a cowboy, we've got these two who are going to move forward now." He waved at Max and Luc, continuing his statement. "They're going to help you if you really need them. So, good luck, ladies, the little pigs are going to appear in a minute so grab you one. There's one or two for each of you so just because one gets away there's another one out there. So, have fun and go for it."

Sheriff Brady gave them a hand wave, then that was their signal to move forward more than they had on his first call. So, they headed in that direction. One on one side and the other on the other side of the large arena.

Wow, his brain yelled when he saw Applegate Thornton and Stanley Orr amble out onto the arena. Then App reached for the rod, ready to lift it and let the greased-up critters explode into the arena while Stanley waved them onward.

Sheriff Brady looked toward the grinning old fellas, then at the ladies as he stepped close to the fence, lifted his hand and said with a grin, "Let the fun begin."

He stepped out of the way as Applegate yanked the gate open and the greasy *little* pigs raced for freedom. App and Stanley laughed and waved their arms making sure the wild greasy pigs charged toward the ladies.

Luc didn't know exactly what to do because it was a wild scene as the piglets charged toward the ladies— why in the world did they race *toward* them and not away from the ladies? Then he remembered that the ladies had to dip their hands into something on their way into the arena. Sweet syrup that attracted the pigs. So not only were the ladies going to be greasy and muddy, they were going to be smelly. Oh, wow, what a night.

His gaze shot to Izzy, who looked stunned as three pigs—the biggest in the bunch—charged toward her. He had to stop himself from urging his horse into action but managed to hold back. Good thing because he saw she was ready to grab one. Ready, but just had to choose which one to dive for before it ran over her.

His gaze shot to the other ladies, who were all grinning like the party had started, they had done this before. His gaze shot back to Izzy as she dove for one of the pigs. She actually *dove* for it, grabbed it by the neck and instantly the foot-and-a-half tall bundle of muscle tossed her to the ground, jumped on her, over her, and there she lay.

A wild yell erupted on the other side of the arena, drawing his alarmed gaze—there were women and pigs, racing, wallowing, and squeaking with glee. Over where Max was, those four gals were rolling in the mud laughing and screaming and kicking those colorful boots and waiting for Max to ride to the rescue.

Max, he just sat there in the saddle, his wrists crossed together over the saddle horn, laughing as he watched the show. Those ladies were having fun, no doubt about it.

His gaze shot back to Izzy, who was now on her hands and knees, muddy as a pig that had just rolled in the mud pit. Her eyes glared, and there was no laughter on her face, it was fury. She sprang to her feet, shot her gaze to him, then to several of the little greasy pigs, and then the woman charged.

He laughed at her frenzied, aggressive crossing of that arena as the entire stands full of watchers roared with laughter. Then she flung her small body into the air, arms outstretched...and landed on the larger piglet. She grabbed it around the neck, spun onto her back which flung the pig's feet straight into the air. The piglet squealed and roared, its legs raking at the sky as she held on. But that greasy pig managed to flip on her, stomped her in the belly—or chest—and that was when Luc spurred his horse forward because he'd seen her face.

Saw the pain as she was stomped in just the right spot. Her arms went limp, and the pig sprang free. But

Izzy went completely limp in the mud, and he couldn't leave her there.

Charging forward like he was racing after a calf, he sprang from the saddle right before the horse reached her, tossed his reins over the horse's neck as soon as he was free, slid on his knees through the mud, his hands reaching out to scoop her upper body from the mud and gently he held her in safety. Those amazing eyes of hers locked on his as she looked up into his and waited for the air to seep back into her struggling lungs.

He gently laid his hand on her chest. "Easy there, it'll come. Believe me, I've been where you are. It will come, just don't struggle. Easy now. It'll be there." And then as if her lungs had suddenly filled, she gasped, hiccupped, and grunted.

And he grinned as she sucked in the first air of the last few moments and her eyes remained locked on his.

He gently patted her back trying to help her as she breathed. Slowly she sucked in her second breath, and he eased her closer against his chest, her shoulder nudging him in the heart like a lightning bolt saying hello.

Focus, Luc! "Come on, it's happening, you're good. Just stay relaxed, Izzy. You can do this. And remember, you almost had him. If he hadn't been a greased-up pig, he'd have been yours." He felt her breathing good and easy as she leaned her head against his shoulder and looked up at him.

And he fought the sudden awareness that smacked him in the chest.

"I don't want a pig. I should have said no. What a fool I was, that's all there is to it."

He couldn't take his eyes off her and needed to see a smile on that troubled face of hers. "But just think how your grannies are up in heaven laughing and cheering you on. They know you did good and did it for them. And they knew you were going to breathe, so remember you, Izzy Cranberry, gave them a great evening."

Suddenly her eyes teared up, she gasped, "Oh, my goodness, you're right." Her words wobbled as did her pretty lips and her eyes closed. "Why, what am I thinking? Yes, you're right, that's why I'm here and what it's all about. Grammy and Gram are having a good evening."

Her eyes reopened but the sadness was gone and joy-filled, gleeful, happy, amazing blue eyes caught his, and he liked what he saw there.

This woman was beautiful, and she was fulfilling a dream for the two people she loved dearly. And in his heart of hearts, he wished he could do that too.

"Yeah, they're having a great night and you are too I think."

Her hand came to his wrist and patted it. "I should have said this before, I should have meant it, thank you. Thank you for everything you've done since our crazy first meeting. You are helping my grammies have a great night. Because whether I want to admit it or not, you are my hero and they loved watching you charge across the arena to save me. I didn't see it happen, but that's the only way you got to my side so quickly. You rode like a champion, jumped off that horse and slid to my rescue. And that was exactly what they wanted to see. So, thank you for making their dream come true."

And then to his horror, she passed out, went limp in his arms and her head drooped against his heart.

CHAPTER THIRTEEN

She woke up in the arms of the cowboy she had been rescued by. The cowboy she knew her grams were happy about. She blinked as she looked up into his concerned eyes. "I don't know why…"

"I don't know either, but you passed out, and I'm glad I was here. The emergency workers are here now too, so I'm going to lay you over on this stretcher they're going to carry you out to the ambulance after they check you out. So just hang in there, hopefully, there is nothing wrong. Hopefully, you were just overwhelmed by everything." He grinned at her. "Just your grams' wish about being rescued by a cowboy coming true."

She couldn't help grinning as she saw the twinkle in his eyes, knowing he was just trying to make her feel better about her grams rooting her on.

"Yeah, so I added to the tale by passing out in the hero's arms."

He nodded. "I guess so, anyway, I'm glad to make their story what they wanted. Now, I'm going to put you on that stretcher, and we'll see how you do. No worries, it's just fiction you know."

"You got that right, but we're giving them a good show." Her words were soft and breathless and there was nothing she could do about it. She told herself it was from the craziness going on inside of her from the little hog jumping on her in just the right spot to knock her breathless. *Crazy*—it had *nothing* to do with how his eyes shined looking at her or the sweet way he talked about her grams.

Anxious and not wanting to pass out again, she yanked her gaze away from his and focused on the female EMT who was smiling at her. Also, the male that was kneeling at her feet. In that moment they slipped her onto the stretcher.

"Now, you just relax, we're going to take your vitals," the EMT gal said as she listened to her heart.

Izzy prayed her heart was okay, but just to make sure, she kept her eyes on the lady and refused to let her gaze go back where it wanted to go. To the cowboy still kneeling by her side making sure she was okay and making her grammies smile from up above.

After a few minutes of being checked out and everything being okay, they let her sit up then helped her stand up and thank goodness Luc stepped back and let the EMT duo take control…meaning she didn't have to feel his touch or look into his eyes again.

Miraculously she was steady as she stood, just like she was supposed to be.

"Alright," the female EMT said. "We're going to let you go back and let this rodeo continue. However, we believe you shouldn't go back into the arena to catch that pig again." She smiled, patted her on the arm as the male let her do the talking while he then pushed the stretcher across the arena and through the open gates.

"Thank y'all," Izzy said. "I'm done, so no worries. I'm not a farmer, a rancher or the catcher of anything, or a rodeo queen. I was just the entertainment for the evening."

"Me either, I just work this and don't participate, but I see a lot of people having a good time doing this and enjoying themselves after...and even getting married. Good luck to you and..." She leaned in. "Maybe you might want to let that handsome cowboy who's been standing by your side help you get out of this arena."

She looked at the grinning lady. "Maybe I don't want to."

The EMT gal grinned. "I don't see why not. That is one good-looking cowboy, but better yet he's a stand-by-you kind of man. And that is worth far more than looks."

Her glance went to him, and she had to agree on everything the EMT said. He was good-looking, and he had come to her rescue.

His lips hitched, and he held out his elbow. "I didn't hear a word, but if you'll allow me, I'll escort you off this muddy arena and get you somewhere you can clean up and maybe watch the rodeo instead of getting trampled by an enthusiastic piglet."

She grinned, unable not to. "Okay, let's do this

but—" She looked at the grinning EMT gal. "You just better stay there because this time if I pass out again, you'll be partly to blame."

The EMT gal grinned. "Sure thing, I'll watch you and this cowboy walk away and then I'll head out at the end. Now go on, an entire arena of people are waiting for you to give them the sign you're okay."

And so, she slid her arm through Luc's, her cowboy hero, and together to the cheers of the rodeo fans, they walked out of the arena and to her startled surprise, Luc pulled his Stetson off and waved it to the crowd—which got more cheers as they walked across the arena and through the gate. At the gate, a grinning Applegate held the gate open for them.

And all the ladies, muddy and grinning, watched them go. Boy, what an experience that she was never going to do again. Grams or no grams she was *never* chasing a greasy pig in a rodeo arena ever again.

Then as Luc placed his hat back on his head and patted her muddy hand that was weaved through his, she couldn't help but look up at him.

He winked at her. "Just doing my duty. You

hangin' in there?"

"Oh, yeah, just ready to cut loose and sit down in all this mud and who knows what else that's clinging to me."

He chuckled. "Right, got the hint, so look you're in luck, there comes your ladies and they'll get you all cleaned up."

She looked and there stood Lacy, Molly, Esther Mae, Norma Sue, and Adela—and instantly she was engulfed and swept away from the cowboy who made her definitely unsteady and had her mind spinning.

Sunday morning Luc stood beside Bob in the choir. Yep, when they found out he had a tenor voice and enjoyed singing all by his lonesome on the range, they hadn't let him not join the choir. There were a lot of cowboys, but there were some ladies too. In the middle of the pack was Lilly. The small, short-haired gal who was married to Cort Wells had a voice like an angel. Esther Mae and Norma Sue sang too, and sweet Adela was the piano player, and that little lady could make those keys sing.

Today they sang "Amazing Grace," and as he sang, he forced himself not to let his gaze drift to the one lady in the audience who drew his attention.

He knew exactly where she was sitting. He knew she didn't want him looking at her, getting rumors roaring more than they already were, so he didn't.

She'd only been here a few short days, and he couldn't get her off his mind. When they finished that song, they began the song that always sent his world spinning. "When We All Get To Heaven" made his gut wrench, and he had to focus on the words, knowing that one day, *one day*, they'd all be together. Those he'd lost before and those he had no plans to get to know better. He could never, would never, take the chance of losing anyone he loved ever again.

But that song, it played loud and clear…"When We All Get To Heaven." He knew one day, no matter whether they wanted to see him or not, he'd be reunited with those he'd loved then lost. As long as he and they all knew the Lord, and they did. His adoptive parents and his adoptive sister he'd lost all together in one slamming disaster that only he, the driver, had survived.

How, how could God ever help him get through just the moments like this when he was doing okay and then the pain slammed into him like a cement wall?

Unable to help himself, his gaze went to the beauty standing there in the pew facing him, and her gaze met his. In her eyes he saw joy, not pain. Unable to help himself, he kept his eyes glued to hers as the song finished. He was then able to walk off the stage with the other choir members into their seats in the pews, and he was able to listen to Preacher Chance.

The cowboy preacher then took the pulpit and Luc sat there in the pew beside a herd of single cowboys, but who did the preacher's gaze land on? Luc.

"My verse of the day is Isaiah six verse three. God laid it on my heart today and it's taking the place of what I'd planned to speak on." Then he nodded slightly to Luc. "*Give them a beautiful headdress instead of ashes, the oil of gladness instead of mourning the garment of praise instead of faint spirit.*"

Luc's heart tightened, was Pastor Chance speaking straight to him? It felt as if he looked into Luc's head and his heart knew what he suffered. It suddenly struck him hard, had Pace told him his story.

But Pace had assured him when Luc had told him his story that night sitting by the fire that Luc's story wasn't his to share, but it was Luc's to come to terms with. To let go of and let God handle it. Luc knew that Pace hadn't even told his sweet wife the pain that Luc had suffered. He trusted Pace. Still, Preacher Chance finished the verse and then finally looked at the congregation.

In that moment, Luc just happened to be sitting in the pew that was one behind Izzy and across the aisle. Therefore, when Izzy glanced over her shoulder slightly and met his gaze, it told him somehow she had recognized those words had been meant for him.

He looked away, unable to hold her gaze because the last thing he wanted was her sympathy. He didn't want anything from her.

Actually, he was afraid of her and that struck him hard.

He'd lost everyone he loved, everyone who meant something to him, in one swift crash. Everyone who had ever loved him, the people who had taken him in, loved him as their own. Brought him up feeling included instead of shunned and thrown away. And in one blink of an eye, they were all gone.

But thank God, they'd known the Lord, and so he knew where they were. Knew one day he and his sister would hug, together with their parents and Jesus.

He fought off emotion, and as soon as the service was over, he got up and quickly made it to the side exit. He walked out into the sunshine and straight across the grass to his truck, beating everyone. He got in, cranked it and drove out the exit and down the road. Unable to let anyone see the pain he dealt with.

It was time to work with his bull.

He hoped, prayed, that Mammoth gave him a hard time. He needed it.

Needed something—a kick in the gut. In the head, *something*, anything to take his mind off his past.

CHAPTER FOURTEEN

Outside the church, Izzy looked for Luc, but he wasn't there. She was surrounded by sweet ladies and the cutest children, but her mind was on Luc.

She'd heard it as the song played and his amazing tenor voice wobbled, and his eyes grew troubled as he continued the song. She'd seen the sadness and heard it in his voice as he forced himself to sing the song.

The song her grams had loved.

The song that had been sung at both their funerals because they loved it so much. "When We All Get To Heaven" was their song, and she knew that one day it would happen, and they'd all be there reunited because they'd all come to know the Lord before they died. Oh, it was going to be a reunion with them at the feet of the

Lord.

She'd lost her mom and dad early, and one day she'd see them again—her grams made sure she knew this and that it was a gift from the Lord to reunite in heaven. Her grams had kept them alive in her mind, and she loved them desperately just for that. Though she'd been barely three when they'd died together in a car accident, she knew almost everything there was about her parents, their troubles, and how their love helped them overcome anything together. Until the accident took them away together. And left her in the loving arms of her grams. She teared up thinking about it but wouldn't let it sweep her into sorrow. She'd been blessed to have her grams to help her and knew there were so many who didn't have that support and love in hard times and good times. Being loved was not something to take for granted, and so many did just that.

She never would. She was oh, so grateful for her brief time as a toddler with her parents and would never forget that one day when they all met up in heaven, they'd celebrate.

But earlier, staring at Luc, there had been such

sadness that had swept over him, visible sadness that maybe she was the only one who'd seen it because she'd been trapped by his handsome face. His kind heart drew her no matter how much she didn't want to be drawn to him. After last night especially, he'd saved her, held her...

And because of that she'd seen the look of deep sadness and anguish and had to know what it was about those beautiful words of that amazing song that changed him from smiling one moment to sadness, making her heart ache for him.

Now that heart of hers wanted to walk quickly away from all the laughing, happy children running and playing about her and their mothers. Molly, Lacy, and Rose, the smiling prickly pear jelly maker, who stood with them and others of the ladies who'd found love here in this small town full of lonesome cowboys.

Was this man who lived down the road lonesome? Sad was for certain but did that sadness have something to do with what was missing in his life? Standing there to the side, older than the others but not too old. There were just so many outside the church having a good time, and it was true that Mule Hollow might have had a shortage of women to marry all their cowboys but despite that fact, with all those ranches full of cowboys, there were still a lot of single cowboys this town was still determined to marry off.

The town was flourishing with life and love, and she felt it. She knew why her grams loved everything about this town. Tears welled in her eyes—she didn't need to be crying. No one here needed to see her cry. She blinked, looked away and knew it was time to go home.

She needed a jog. A long jog, something she hadn't done since she arrived. She'd met up with a rattlesnake, a huge bull, and a cowboy neighbor. But a jog she hadn't had, and today was the day. When she jogged, she felt energy, her heart was well, her life was good, and she jogged for the joy of it. It helped her stay healthy and could help her live like her grams. They'd lived their long lives partly because it was inherited from their ancestors. But they hadn't been raised on candy, high sugar, and junk. No, they'd been raised straight off of rich farmland produce, and it had benefitted them. Good food that their grandpas and grandmas had raised them on. They'd taught her that, so she tried to eat healthy. With as little candy as she could, but she had a sweet tooth too. Exactly the sweetness her grams loved due to the Molly Popp articles about Mule Hollow. Banana LaffyTaffy was a love of hers, to pop it in her mouth, chew slowly and enjoy the awesome sweet taste.

It was the same thing that Samantha the donkey loved—the donkey she still had to meet. Lilly, her owner, sat up there in the choir and sang with the men just like her grams had told her she did. And now, across the way was the little boy who'd helped rescue his mom, Molly, and bring him into the world. And now, they were a beautiful family, and it touched her heart. Her grams had loved the Christmas story of his parents, who were matchmade by Samantha. And yes, she understood her grams hoped something would happen for her while she was here. But she just couldn't give in to a dream like that.

Mule Hollow was her grams' dream, not hers. She was simply here fulfilling their dream of visiting the people and the town that had given them happiness in their last years…and yes, a hope that she would be one of the gals who came and fell in love with a cowboy. But she wasn't going to do that.

I have my own dreams, she repeated in her suddenly vague mind. She was going to move to a big city and open a big salon that would touch a larger crowd than here. She was a great hairdresser, and she knew it. She loved giving someone a new look and seeing the sparkle in their eyes when they saw it in the mirror after she was finished. When they saw the cut fit their face, highlighted their eyes, and made their smile widen across their happy face. That was the moment she waited for and loved.

The look of hair could bring out the beauty of anyone just because it made them smile. And that was what she loved about it.

Everyone was beautiful on the inside if they just didn't let the demons and anger of the world tear down the joy that could be there. The joy her grandmothers had instilled in her from the day they'd taken her in after the horrible accident that had taken her parents from her. Life wasn't always perfect, but her sweet grams had taught her that you took what was given to you and you made joy come from it in memory of those you loved.

She smiled at Lacy, who she realized was staring at her. "I'm going to go. It's time for a jog. It's been wonderful, but I'll see you all soon."

Everyone said goodbye to her, and she was glad that the salon was closed on Sunday and Monday, giving her two full days off. She suddenly needed it.

Lacy had said she wanted to keep it that way to give her time to relax because everyone needed time to relax. And so, she would. She took long strides out to the pink caddy that sat there waiting with its top down. She liked the top down and had driven home with it down. She had put it up for the night, but this morning she'd put it back down. And just looking at it made her smile. She was about to feel the breeze on her face. Her hair blew free, her body felt free, she felt free as the wind surrounded her and the blue sky opened up ahead as she drove.

Now, as she sank into the seat and cranked up the caddy, her heart thundered with the roar of the engine, and she smiled again.

How could an ancient pink caddy do that to someone?

But it did, this pink caddy had a way about it, she thought as she backed out and then headed for the road. She turned toward home...home for now, not forever. This pink caddy had brought Lacy Brown and her friend Sheri to town and changed everything. Now, as she drove, she was suddenly so grateful. So, she just drove. Instead of turning down her road when she arrived, she kept on going.

She let her hair blow, hung her left hand out of the side of the car and let her fingers wave in the wind as she carefully drove one-handed along the road. "*Oh, what a beautiful day,*" she said out loud and meant it as the words carried on the breeze.

Her heart lifted, and she found herself smiling. How could a ride with the wind blowing in her face whisk all her problems away in those moments? Give her relief and joy as the miles ticked away? It was wonderful.

She thought about Luc suddenly and on impulse she stomped on the brake and then turned the car around, drove back to their dirt road, and pulled onto the ranch where Luc was living. Unable to stop herself, she parked the car and got out. The man had saved her three times, and in her heart of hearts, she felt like he needed her. There was one thing she'd learned in her life, taught to her by her grams—she wasn't a chicken.

Nope, she wasn't, so she walked toward where she saw him in the arena, heard his voice. She closed her eyes—he had a calming, easy voice right now, and she opened her eyes and slowed her pace hearing his words and knowing he was talking to the angry bull.

She moved to the round arena, cautiously approaching. Not wanting to disturb them since curiosity had the better of her. And there, when she peeked through the metal bars, was the unbelievably handsome cowboy. He stood in the center, his hands by his side. He had a gentle voice as he spoke to the bull that had his huge head down and raked one foot in the dirt. It was staring at Luc with either rage or curiosity. It was evident whatever he was feeling, he wasn't sure about. She watched and prayed he didn't charge.

"Alright, dude. It's our time. You're going to learn not to let that rage that is inside of you overtake the curiosity you have. Just like me, you have to learn to take one moment at a time and learn to listen and adjust. When I talk to you, it's with the hope that you'll learn to know that I'm standing here by your side, but if you want to charge me, you can—but I guarantee you won't do it again. You'll learn that sometimes there are paths we cannot take. And I can't have you trying to hurt someone. One minute you're good and one minute you're angry. Believe me, I get it. I live with it every day. Like today. That song—yeah, I'll see them one day, but why them and not me? Why did they have to die and me keep on living? Why couldn't they still be here?"

Her heart ached. He'd lost someone he loved—sounded like he'd lost more than one. He'd lost like she had, people he loved. He sounded like he knew them well, was it the woman he'd loved? Her heart ached for him. She'd been so young when her mom and dad died. She had small memories, and if she'd been four, she might have remembered more about them. Now, mostly what she remembered was what her grams had told her. How she was loved and cherished and how she'd blessed them coming late into her parents' lives when they'd thought they'd never have one of their own. She'd blessed them and then lost them, but thank God for her grams who had lived to be so old and full of love.

Her grams had told her longevity was in their family and she could live as long as them, maybe as old as Great-Gram at a hundred and six. And if she did, they wanted her to live for all of them, knowing she was loved and to spread that love with a smile and a heart of gold.

Standing there looking across that arena, her heart thundered.

What was she doing?

That was what she couldn't let go of. She had a good life to live for her parents that she'd lost. As she stood there looking at Luc, her heart ached for him.

What had happened to him? What had put that sound in that wonderful voice of his? That voice that she sometimes heard when she didn't want it to, rang in her ears.

She knew now, she had to find out who he'd lost.

CHAPTER FIFTEEN

Luc saw Mammoth's eyes pivot to the fence behind him, and he knew instantly they weren't alone. Calmly, he turned, not wanting to startle the bull that had been listening intently to him. When he found her standing there looking through the fence at him, his mind instantly reeled.

"Hello, you know how to sneak up on people."

"I didn't want to interrupt. How's Mammoth doing?"

He wondered what all she'd heard. Needed her not to have heard too much. "He's doing better, he has his moments. Like we all do."

She leaned against the railing and smiled through the space and his insides wobbled. "Yeah, you know I do, and now I know—I mean, I know you too have moments."

She'd heard. He sighed, turned from Mammoth and strode across the arena. She watched him, and he tried not to let it affect him anymore as he opened the gate and walked through. "So, you're out and about today. It's your free afternoon."

"Yes, and well, I...I was going to try and see you after church, but you disappeared."

"You were hunting me down?"

She smiled, and he didn't know why he was teasing but he couldn't help it. "Yes, I was. I—well, actually I was driving in the pink caddy with the top down, and it's a great day, and I thought maybe you might need a drive too."

He stared at her, and the way her eyes held his, it was as if she was reading him. Pushing, seeking but not wanting to do too much. Cautious. "So, why do you think I might want or need to take a ride?"

She raked a hand through her hair. "Well, Lacy told me that riding in that pink caddy with the top down, letting the wind blow in your eyes and face was a great experience. That it had given her freedom and helped her through hard times and good times, and it was something she thought everyone needed sometimes. Even if it was to ride in your truck with the window down and the breeze blowing in and your hand hanging out feeling the flow through your fingers. Well, little did I know but she was right. It's kind of addictive.

"And honestly—okay, that song that we sang, "When We All Get To Heaven," touches me deeply. I can't wait until I see all the people I love one day. It relieves me knowing that they were all Christians and brought me to know the Lord so one day at the feet of the Lord we'll be together. It gives me joy. But I saw sadness in your face today. Pain when you were singing and…well, as I was driving down the road, feeling the air in my hair, I thought of you. And I don't know why that song affects you that way, but I just felt like I was supposed to—no, I wanted to come and ask you if you would take a ride with me."

He didn't know what to say or feel. Last night had been great, seeing her safe and sound. Today had reminded him why he couldn't let this woman into his life.

"Come for a ride with me. Enjoy the feel of God's air crossing your face, just embracing you, and let the peace flow through you as we drive over the country roads surrounding this amazing Mule Hollow."

He was stunned, floored, enticed, enchanted. She had read him like an open book.

Say no.

The words flashed through him, but something in those eyes and those gentle words and that kind spirit that was reaching out to him was undeniable. "Okay, sounds like a great plan. If you're sure."

Her eyes misted and her smile spread across her face as if it was a new day. A new dawning. And his chest squeezed tight at the thought.

"I think it's a great idea. And like you told me last night when I was laying there crumpled on the ground, my grams were smiling and having a great time. And they're doing the same thing right now for you."

"Maybe so." He felt a nudge in his gut. It was a nudge he resisted. He didn't want to feel. In one swift, blunt moment he had lost everyone he cared for. And he had been driving. Hadn't been his fault, but he hadn't been able to prevent it. Or forget it. And he could never ever face something like that again. So, he'd hidden out. Hidden out in the boonies until finally Pace's invitation had struck him hard, and here he was looking into the eyes of this stunningly beautiful lady, inside and out.

She felt energized and erratic—crazy and sporadic—and as she approached the pink caddy knowing he was coming with her, she did what she'd been thinking about doing. She put her hands on the closed door of the pink caddy, and like she'd watched Lacy do, she put her weight on her hands and arms then swung her feet over the door and in a flash—not as graceful as Lacy could do it—she landed into the seat in a rough slam.

Then she met the startled, grinning face of Luc, and she laughed. "It wasn't as good as Lacy, but it felt good."

"Well, it looked like it might have hurt," he said, his voice rattled with laughter trying to get out as he stood there and stared. "You might not need to do it again."

"Well, actually, I'm not going to stop. I'm going to keep trying until I get as good at it as Lacy. For her, it's just a movement that fits her. A freedom, so yeah, I'm going to keep working at it. How about you, going to give it a try?"

He laughed out loud now, which was great after seeing him earlier. His laughter was heart-punching wonderful.

"I think I'll just climb in. My legs are a lot longer and my boots are a lot heavier and I...well, I don't want you having to call the ambulance on me or anything." She laughed as he opened the door and slid into the seat beside her. Still holding his hat in his hands, he held her gaze, and her heart is what slammed to the ground.

"I guess we'll go," she said, thankful she got the words out as she yanked her gaze from his to the steering wheel, turned the engine on and then giving him a glance, she smiled. "Put your seat belt on. Here we go."

And so, they drove. Down the road, hung a right and headed away from town this time, and she had no idea where they were going to end up.

They rode along the country road that wound through the country away from Mule Hollow. The road had curves and hills boarded by barbed wire fences, large oak trees mixed with open pastures, and many, many cattle grazing beyond the fences.

Luc was conflicted by his choice to come along. But when she'd hit the main road, he'd realized that he had no idea how she planned to drive this pink Cadillac.

But, she'd shot him that grin, told him to fasten his seatbelt then gunned it the moment she'd turned onto the paved road—not that they were over speeding but, they were doing the top of the chart in, as the ladies called it, the topless pink caddy. And his hair was hatless and the wind blowing over the top of the windshield had his-semi short hair dancing—but he didn't dare put his hat on, he gripped it tightly and enjoyed the ride.

The wind swirled like crazy, but instead of feeling worried that Izzy couldn't drive, it was obvious she could—she had two hands on the wheel and her eyes were on the road. She was in control, or as in control as one could be, so he relaxed. He'd learned that some things couldn't be controlled completely, but sometimes the endings weren't in our control.

Still, though he knew this first hand, in this moment, he actually relaxed, even if he was with the beautiful Izzy Cranberry.

In that moment the woman shot him a smile then looked back at the road. But that smile doused him like a pitcher of sweet cranberry juice, and he didn't mind.

Didn't mind at all.

He should worry about that, yeah, he should, but with the wind blowing through his hair, in that moment, he wasn't worried. He just let enjoyment fill him—not for long. He wouldn't let it happen.

Let what happen?

He wasn't letting anything happen. But there wasn't anything that said he couldn't enjoy a few moments. And she was right—he'd needed this.

And those miles they traveled together, without saying anything, were great. He felt the joy she felt showing in her smile as she drove. She concentrated on driving, and he concentrated on the trip but kept her happy face in his vision. He didn't let her know he was watching her. No, he kept his head turned toward the road, but his gaze was to the side locked on her.

Why?

He didn't want to know the answer. Didn't want to know the reason for the feelings he'd never known before racing through him from just spending time with her.

Right *now*, all he wanted was to feel the relief that she'd known riding in this pink Cadillac would bring him. Songs played in his head, an old tune popped into his head in that moment, one that meant a lot to him. *Riding in My Car*—only after the words played in his head did it hit him they weren't the title to the song playing in his head. Growing up, hearing his dad singing the lyrics to *Fire* to his mom and then sweeping her into his arms, tilting her down and kissing her there in the kitchen. It was a great memory.

Suddenly, he wasn't thinking about his parents or anything other than kissing *Izzy*.

The song talked about riding in a car, but the title was—*Fire*.

And in that moment that's what raged through him as Izzy shot him another questioning look.

"What's flying inside that head of yours?" she asked.

What was it about this woman and music? "Well," he said, over the wind, and laughed. "The radio isn't on, but I have songs playing in my head."

She laughed. "*Me too.* It's crazy. I feel like I'm sitting in Sam's Diner and all those old songs have hitched a ride with me in this pink caddy. Christian songs and old songs that make me smile. And some that have such deep meanings they turn on smiles and teardrops too."

She was looking back at the road, but her words slammed into him unexpectedly and he froze.

She looked him again. "Look, I know at church 'When We All Get To Heaven' made me happy but not you. Sorry." She must have seen his emotions in his expression. "Only talk about that one if you want to. Right now, what songs are dancing around in that brain of yours, making you smile?"

Relief shot through him and he didn't waste time thinking. "You know that old song, *Fire?* The one that talks about riding in a car?" He couldn't stop himself as he sang words that were playing in his mind. He couldn't remember all the lyrics, but the song talked about riding in a pink caddy and they were in the caddy.

She slapped the steering wheel with her palm. "Great timing on that one. Riding in *this* car is fun, and I'm loving it. Especially with you singing."

"Thanks," he chuckled, feeling some relief. "It's got a great tune to it."

She slowed the car, not to a stop but just creeping along. "So, liking that song tells me you're not just a country and western music fan."

"You're right, my mom enjoyed all kinds of music. Happy songs especially, the ones that had joy in them and made you smile. Dad was the country music lover but he liked country songs that dug deep and touched his heart. *Not* country songs about booze, loving a woman then looking for a woman on the side. Dad wasn't into those, and I'm not either." It was true. "Dad always said he only had eyes for one woman, my mom. So, why would he want to listen to troubling songs and make her think he had other women on his mind. He was a good man."

She'd practically stomped the brake. "That's wonderful of him and your mom. Teaching you to love songs with happiness and meaning to them, I love those kind too." She grinned at him. "Songs that spread joy through my heart. And are fun." She sang the words, "*We're in this car.*"

Luc grinned and joined in... *"I'm singin' with a spunky gal."*

She laughed at his off pace verse and added, *"And a hunky cowboy."*

He rolled his eyes, they laughed and their song went on. Each of them creating a verse that didn't have exactly the same tune, but one of its own. And she was good at it...and through his head lyrics only he could hear begin to play...

She was fun.

She helped ease the heartache and pain inside him...

Float away on the breeze…

And when those beautiful eyes of hers met his—the words played in his head as her eyes met his and instantly a grin busted across his face.

A huge grin, a smile bigger than he'd smiled in a very, *very* long time.

CHAPTER SIXTEEN

She was enjoying the ride and the singing. It was a fun blast that she hadn't expected. What *was it* about this pink Cadillac?

She didn't really want to talk about why she'd picked him up because that smile and his singing voice were amazing.

And fun. And what a coincidence they liked some of the same music from their past.

Past was a tricky thing.

Good past. Bad past…making your own past.

Her mind went from riding in the caddy to something her great-gram had told her that last time Izzy got to sit beside her bed and hold her hand. Gram could no longer get out of bed and was almost unable to see anymore. But as she lay there beneath the white sheet propped up on her pillows, she'd hold that small boney hand out. That hand with fingernails Izzy kept trimmed back for her and painted soft colors.

"Izzy," she'd said, that last night, gently squeezing Izzy's hand. "I had a long life. A hard life that involved a hundred and six, almost a hundred and seven *amazing* years. I could look at the bad things, the hard times through those years, but everyone has them. Me, well God had a plan for me to outlive almost everyone I knew but my sweet daughter—your Grammy, and you, my Izzy girl. There was a reason for it, maybe its for me to tell you to love the Lord. To follow *His* path for your life."

Izzy's heart had tangeled up at those words. "You've touched many, many lives Gram, not just me."

"Good," she said softly. "You know your Grammy, is going to join me in heaven just a little after I get there because I've lived so very long. But it's all God's timing and He blessed *me* to let be here with the two of you and let us watch you grow into the woman you are."

"Ohh, Gram," Izzy had said, her heart hurting. "I'm

the blessed one."

Gram's lips softened and her eyes held hers. "Remember, dear girl, one day we're all going to see each other again. So, let the good things that happened in your life take over and be thankful to the Lord. My mama taught me to love the Lord and I hope I helped show you the way." She grinned, it lit her fading eyes bright, and Izzy's heart swelled.

"Oh, Gram, how I love you. You've shown me the way. Shown me so much love, and if I can just live half of the happy life you've shown me, I'll be grateful. If I ever find love and decide to have babies, I assure you I'll pass on to my babies my love of the Lord taught to me by you, Grammy, and, in their short time with me, my mom and dad."

Tears in her eyes, Izzy added, "Thank y'all for telling me about my dad. He was kind of a wild man when he met my mom, but my mom made him know that he wanted to be a better man, and so that's what he did. He came to know the Lord, and so now I know that, like all of you, I'll also see him again right there with Mom. This time not in caskets side by side but in the joy of heaven. It's going to be great."

Sweet Gram nodded, patted her hand, then rested her head on the pillow, closed her eyes, and, with a smile on her face, she'd said, "Oh, yes, oh, *what a day* it will be."

Izzy glanced at Luc but didn't talk about that now. If the time was right and he wanted to talk about living and death, then she would share. Instead she said, "This is beautiful country. Look at the area over there."

"Yeah, this is Cort and Lilly Wells's place. You know, where Samantha the donkey lives." At his words, she pressed down hard on the brake. Stopped right there in the middle of the road.

"This is where *Samantha* lives?"

"It sure is, she's out there somewhere. She's a roamer. Pull in. They're heading off in a couple of weeks, and I'm going to come over while they're gone and look after things for them."

"That's nice of you. She invited me out to meet Samantha because she knew my grams loved her."

"Then turn in right up there."

She didn't hesitate as she pressed the gas pedal,

turned onto the dirt road, and hung a left at the ranch entrance. And there standing beside the fence into the backyard stood the short, fat donkey. Samantha. Izzy smiled and her heart pumped with delight. At that moment Lilly came out the door and waved. As she stopped at the gate, she handed Samantha a small piece of yellow that the donkey took, grinned, then walked away chewing happily.

"Banana LaffyTaffy."

He chuckled. "Yep, that donkey loves that taffy."

"So do I. My grams got me hooked on it, so now I have to only give it to myself as a treat. A reward for finishing up a task."

"Good idea. Come on, park, and let's hop out."

Lilly agreed, "Y'all come on out."

And to all their voices, Samantha did a tiptoe dance move and headed their way. In that moment a hairy little brown dog came rushing around the end of one of the long stables, his eyes beamed, and he raced so fast his hair streamed in the wind. Lucky—she knew instantly from her grams talk of the dog named Loser now Lucky.

They hurried out of the car, and Lilly gave her a

hug. "I've been waiting for you. And so have they." She waved at Samantha and Lucky, who had practically screeched to a halt beside the grinning donkey, and they both watched her with sparkling curious eyes.

"I'm glad to be here, and oh, they are so real...I mean exactly like my grams imagined." She stepped forward and started petting Samantha's forehead and bent down to rub Lucky's head as he placed his short-legged feet on her calf and grinned up at her for attention too.

"You brought a cowboy with you," Lilly said, drawing Izzy's gaze from the animals to the smiling face of the curly dark-haired lady.

"Well, he happens to live down the road from me, and I was going for a drive, and he's kind of new in town too, though I know now he knows y'all. But he'd never ridden in the pink caddy, so I asked him if he wanted a ride. And you know how it goes, he wanted to go riding in the pink Cadillac."

Lilly laughed. "Oh, goodness, it never gets old."

Izzy was glad she could make it funny since Luc had crossed his arms and was grinning and letting her and Lilly carry on the conversation. "We were driving along enjoying the day and suddenly your ranch came into view, and he told me who owned it when I asked, and of course I knew this awesome donkey and pup lived here and couldn't pass it up. Then he told me y'all were about to go out of town and he was going to watch out for these two."

"Yes, week after next. We're so glad you're going to check on them for us over the week and know that just keeping these two in line will be the hardest part of your day." She chuckled, reached out and rubbed Samantha's neck. "She's a sweetie but getting older, so I don't think she'll be breaking out and roaming like she used to."

"If she decides to test me like Mammoth, I'll find her, so no worries."

Samantha took that moment to sit on her rear, cock her head to the side and let out a loud heehaw. They all laughed.

Lucky popped his paws on her neck and let out a bark.

"I think they're telling you they're going to give

you a run for your money," she said, chuckling as she looked at the donkey. "I've heard a lot about you, Samantha the donkey. You liked to get in trouble and at the same time bring happiness."

Samantha let out another heehaw then popped up to all four hooves and sashayed to the barn with Lucky following across the yard and into the giant stable with a large opening.

Lilly smiled and watched. "You'll see in a moment what they're doing. She obviously decided while we were distracted talking that it was a good time to go sneak herself a treat. Now, don't think because we know what she's doing that we always do. That donkey has a mind of her own and it works like a God-given gift. It did for me and Cort. And yes, she loves her life and so does Lucky."

Then a tall horse, a glamorous horse, came trotting from the barn, his tail high as he let out a whinny and trotted gracefully toward the gate that led to a pasture.

Izzy chuckled. "She let that beauty out and is eating his feed."

"Yes, but we are prepared these days. We let her

get the want to sneak a horse out and steal their feed, but we make sure we have the latch enabled on the horse we want her to let out. She can't get all the stalls opened anymore. But I just couldn't take away all her fun, so we came up with this solution. And we found out that the horses are similar, loving the thought that they are out sneaking around and running free. It works for all of us."

"That's good for me to know," Luc said, grinning.

Izzy laughed. "That's brilliant. Oh, and look, she got what she wanted," she gasped and clapped her hands together in delight as the donkey came trotting from the barn with what looked like a piece of charcoal hanging from her mouth. Not exactly the color but the look.

"Yes, she got her cube out of the bucket after she let the horse out and saw there was no feed in the bucket."

"That's a great idea. She looks happy." Izzy loved it. "I'm so glad I got to see this. My grams loved every article about Samantha and getting to meet her in the story of you and Cort—not that there was a lot written after the first story that got y'all all tangled up. But she always manages to let people know there're happy endings in Mule Hollow."

Lilly smiled. "Yes, she does. And I'm not the one who got aggravated. That was the one Luc is working for. Those two, Pace and Sheri, tried to pull one over on the matchmakers and it backfired on them in a wonderful way. And now, it's brought Luc to Mule Hollow. And you too. Life has a way of spinning out of control. I have to head in and check on my napping kids, but Luc, when you come out to watch over everything, maybe bring Izzy."

Luc's gaze slid to hers and he nodded. "If she wants to. We'll see. Now, we'll head out, and no worries about anything here. I've talked with Cort, and everything is set up. Y'all have a great trip."

Within minutes they'd all said goodbye and then Luc and Izzy were back in the caddy and headed back to the drive. Her mind rolled, and she knew once again something inside of her had shifted a little bit.

She focused on the ride and the time they'd just shared and despite the urge to find out what it was that hurt him so much, she couldn't.

CHAPTER SEVENTEEN

After being at the ranch, they were driving down the road when Izzy looked over at Luc. "You're going to have an adventure watching out over Samantha and Lucky while they're gone." It wasn't a question, she just had so much to say. She fought it hard, but she had a hope that was driving her crazy.

"Yep, when the time comes, I'll be driving over here every day checking up on Samantha and Lucky. And riding the property one day to make sure everything's good with the horses and cattle. I'll be checking on the house down the road too, where Lilly grew up with her three grandmothers. Where Cort and Lilly's love story began—according to what I've heard. Lilly was raised by her grams like you."

"Yes, my grams pointed that out to me. The difference was her three grams hadn't had good relationships and had no use for men. Something Lilly had to overcome. All she had was a friendship with Samantha growing up." She took her eyes off the road again. "But my grams didn't try to keep me from finding someone. They were and still are rooting for me to find the man meant for me." *Why did I say that?* "I'm not looking right now."

"Me either. I'm not looking for love. I have too much in my past that keeps me from wanting something like that. Until I came here, I hadn't seen so much matchmaking. Unlike you, who heard all about it from your grams, I only knew Pace talked about it and wanted me here. When I got here and started playing checkers with App and Stanley and listening to all the stories, only then did I know completely what this town is built on.

"Pace hadn't told me how much went into keeping this town on the map. But seeing all the happy cowboys and their wives now and all the cowboys coming here to work knowing they might be matched up, tells me it's all okay. I'm still not looking and still running into trouble, well, it's something to watch. I knew why Pace wanted me here. I knew, like your grams were hoping for you, that Pace was hoping I would find someone or what I needed. In all honesty, I have. I like the town, the people, and the fact that I can feel God is here even in the hard times. But even though I know Him, my heart can't open up completely. I'm just telling you that. I know you've said you're not opening your heart. You're going to live your grams' dream for a little while and then move on to fulfill *your* dream. I get that. For me, I hid out in Idaho and Montana. Hid out on those huge ranches' back areas, and then I came here and found out that I can live life among other people. I can have my own goals, not theirs, and enjoy watching everyone else seek their dreams and I can pray for them. Not be one of them. I pray they'll find love and happiness and that…that they won't lose everyone in one stinkin' instant."

Her heart ached as his words slammed into her. Her thoughts went back to her grams who, even in the end, were happy with the life they'd lived, and she'd held each one's hand as they'd left this earth and entered heaven. What had happened to him?

Unable to help herself, she pulled the car over on the side of the road, and there among the bluebonnets, the yellow daisies, and the sunflowers beneath the sparkling late afternoon blue skies, all of it spoke happiness.

But between them, she felt a huge connection of sadness but in a different way. For her, she could still smile. But this man—"Okay, you have to tell me what happened in your life to make you so deeply sad. I was holding Gram's and Grammy's hand when each of them passed into heaven. My great-grandma, my gram, was in a bed for several years and couldn't see very well, so I always got close when talking with her. Like I told you before, she was almost one hundred and seven. Grammy, her daughter, died two years later and had been feeling unstable for four years."

"They were glad you were with them."

"Yes, but I was too. Me and Clover, her tiny Chihuahua. Adorable ancient dog loved to sing along with Grammy and always sat in her lap when they sang. She started singing and he'd sing along making the most amazing yelps, whines, and howls in tune and rhythm." She smiled, couldn't help it, the memory was so vivid and memorable.

"His favorite was the old song, "She'll Be Coming Round the Mountain" She chuckled despite the sadness at the thought of hearing Clover and Grammy singing. "On that Fourth of July, I was the one who cooked the chili dogs, and we ate them, had a good time and after the fireworks were over, we sat there together and watched the sparkling lights of God in that dark sky. Then I helped Gram into bed, and I started cleaning the kitchen."

She paused again for strength, and he just watched her, sadness, knowing in his eyes. "Suddenly I heard a noise and rushed into Gram's room. She was sitting up in bed, her Clover was standing beside her at alert. I got to her, and she took my hand and then she died of a heart attack. One minute she was with me smiling and the next she was in heaven having a family reunion. And one day I'll be there too."

She saw the pain in Luc's eyes. He reached out and placed his hand on hers.

She took a tearful breath. "Luc, I'm going to see them again. And until then, I'm going to play here for them, then I'm going to open a salon in a city that calls to me, and like Lacy, I'm going to share His love." Her tears welled up. "Sorry I cried talking about it, but these aren't tears of sadness. Yes, I miss them, but I know where they are so these are tears of happiness. But I want to know why you have such a sadness inside of you. God put you on my heart as I watched you singing, and I can't get you off of my mind. I know something wasn't good in your life, and though I was out driving, God slammed you into my head, and I turned the car around and came back, knowing that was what I was supposed to do. I'm here if you need to talk. I'm a hairstylist; I'm licensed to touch. There is something about a touch that gets people to talk. Not everyone has someone to talk to, so a hairstylist comes in handy. But you can tell me to hush and drive, and I will. After all, I'm in the pink Cadillac," she sang the last words to the tune.

His eyes had turned troubled, but at those song notes, the corner of his lip hitched up slightly. "Maybe there is magic to riding in this car. It shows you that anything can be used by God. An old pink caddy, an old red truck, a new Cadillac, anything can be used by the Lord. A hairstylist, a neighbor, a gal getting stuck in the pasture with a rattlesnake—"

"A cowboy riding up and saving the day," she added with a smile and a thundering heart.

He nodded. "A happy cowboy glad he was there that day because of a stubborn bull that likes to run and romp and not behave. I have to tell you that I feel bad having him all locked in now that I'm thinking about it. I'm thankful for that day and even the day he got out of the pasture and made you crash into that fence and tree. God protected you and gave me the opportunity to meet you in a different way, in a deeper way. So how can I be mad about that? As soon as I get back, I'm going to let him loose."

"Maybe you need to let yourself loose. Have you thought about that? So, what do you say? You going to let me in? Talk to someone?"

Luc was speechless. Stunned. What a testimony she had and what a way to look at loss. "Look, I don't know if I can talk about it, but I appreciate what you shared with me. Some things are just too hard—"

"Only if you don't try. Sometimes, until you start

speaking about your trials and tribulations, you don't know the relief it can bring you."

He rubbed his forehead, wanting out of the car. "Look, I appreciate the ride and what you tried to do today, but I haven't ever talked about it, and I can't talk about it. Yes, I talked to Pace, but never talked about it before or after. So maybe you should just drive. It's time to go home." Her beautiful eyes dug into him, but then she nodded, shifted the car into drive and off they went. She held her hand out the window and let the breeze blow through it. He was certain it was in hopes that he would do the same, but he didn't. He couldn't.

He'd had a great day. A day he'd *never* forget, but still, he just couldn't go there. And Izzy, she didn't push him, she drove, and though he tried not to, his gaze slid to her. He knew she was purposefully giving him space. She'd spoken what the Lord had laid on her heart, and now she wasn't pushing. She was giving him time, might never ask again and wasn't expecting him to share with her. As they pulled into his drive, his heart was thundering. When was the last time he'd had anyone to talk to?

Anyone to share his heartache and pain? Anybody he'd ever come close to sharing with other than Pace? He'd only shared it with him that night because they'd been sitting at the campfire and Pace had told him he was leaving, and he knew that something deep inside was hurting him. He'd told Luc not to fear because he was about to leave and do what God wanted him to do instead of being a recluse sitting on the ranch like the loner that he was. He was a Christian now and was supposed to share what God had done for him, so he was heading to Mule Hollow. But before he went, he just wanted Luc to know that he needed to share his heartache, just to get it out in the open. But it would always stay with him.

He would never tell anyone. Unlike right now, he had told Pace everything. He'd spilled his heartache, his pain, his loss…spilled it all. And from the day when he'd told Pace he'd move to Mule Hollow till this day, Pace had assured him that he'd told no one what Luc had shared with him on that cold winter night about his past. That the people of Mule Hollow would welcome him with open arms. But for him to be aware that the matchmakers would mark him as someone they could match. But not to worry, if it wasn't meant to be, it wouldn't and that was all up to Luc. So just come and live among people who cared because he knew, unlike him, Luc wasn't really a solitary man. He was hiding out. But like Pace had said, when God called, he'd known it was time to step out. And he'd obeyed, ended up in Mule Hollow and in a miraculous way he'd met his destiny in Sheri.

He looked at Izzy, quiet, her hands still gripping the steering wheel, waiting for him to say something. Suddenly unable to stop himself, he reached over and placed his hand on her shoulder. Tears welled inside his soul and need, need he did not—he capitalized that word inside his head—need he did not want to feel, gripped him.

He had to get out of that car.

But his fingers were on her shoulder. "You pushed the buttons inside me today like they've never been pushed before. And I have to let you know that I'm not turning you aside because I'm mad. I'm not. I'm just— I need time to think, and just so you'll also know, I'll never turn back on the way my mind works. I won't say what happened, I'll never talk about it again. Pace is the only one who knows but thank you. Thank you for taking me on this ride because I can honestly say ridin' in your car without the radio on and without the top up was a great day. But I have a bull waiting out in that arena that I have to set free."

He pulled his hand from her shoulder before he did what his heart was pushing him to do and that was caress her jaw, her face and draw those beautiful eyes to his and those lips—he exited the car. Shut the door behind him.

But he turned back, leaned on the door, both hands gripping it. "You, Izzy Cranberry, are like Molly Popp Jacobs and Lacy Brown Matlock. You're on a mission—" His voice wobbled, so he forced the last words out. "And God is going to use you." With that he turned away and strode toward the corral.

CHAPTER EIGHTEEN

That night after Luc left her sitting in the pink caddy and strode away, Izzy sat alone on the back porch at twilight and prayed.

What a man.

What a hurting man he was. She needed to talk to someone, but she couldn't because she was the one who had tried to pull his pain from him. He hadn't offered it, so she couldn't go and talk about it to anyone. It wasn't her right. If and when there was a moment he could talk, she would be there, and he knew where to find her. But she wasn't going to push him. Maybe she wasn't the one.

But as she sat there in that quiet night with fireflies floating through the air, their sparkle and the quietness of the night, the soft sound of the frogs...it was a magical night. And despite everything in her heart and soul that told her no, she suddenly wished beyond any feeling she had ever felt that Luc Asher was sitting beside her, rocking in this swing. Enjoying the beauty with her, sharing this moment. She wished it like she had never wished anything before.

Unable to stop herself, she got up. She couldn't sit there and think of something that was never going to happen. Something she really didn't want. What was she thinking?

How had her mind gone to such a place? She just wanted to help him. She didn't want to fall in love with him. Her life wasn't here—*what?*

What had she thought?

Love. She wasn't falling in love. No way.

She hadn't even lived here a full week. Yep, her grams were enjoying this. There had to be something about this town. She shut her heart down. She had plans. She had a life, and she was going to live it.

As she headed inside, she yanked her clothes off and got ready for bed like she was heading to war. She lay down and demanded that she go to sleep.

Of course, she didn't.

She lay there. Her mind said, "Take a ride in that pink caddy on this moonlit night."

No. She was not getting in that car tonight. Instead, she lay there. And when her mind went to crazy thoughts about that handsome cowboy down the road from her, she prayed.

She didn't pray for her or them but prayed for him.

She prayed God would help Luc, and if He needed her, then He could use her—might take a shove in the right direction. But no matter what, she wasn't going in the direction she didn't want to go.

She wasn't going back to the thoughts of falling in love.

Nope, no, not going there.

Monday morning, she drove the pink caddy straight out of the yard to the repair shop in Ranger, where her car was being given an estimate on getting fixed. The nice wrecker driver had said when he came to pick it up that it was the best place to take it. So, she drove there, and the appraiser told her it wasn't good. That she'd hit that fence and rammed that tree with just enough force and angle that it had ruined her engine. Basically, he told her it was totaled.

Totaled. How could that be?

She told him to hang on to it. She'd talk to the insurance company, then get back to him. Yes, he'd told her it could be repaired but would cost her a lot and the resale value would be shot. Great. And as she stood outside and called her insurance company, they said exactly what the estimator had said, totaled, and they'd send her a check.

So, here she was having to deal with getting a new car—or vehicle. She had no idea what she wanted, hadn't planned on buying one for a while. So, this would take some deciding. Some thought. You didn't just walk into a car dealership without any thought and buy the first car you saw. She didn't anyway.

She had her grams' house to sell, she had money saved. She could buy a new car but had no idea what. So, she walked away and got into the pink caddy she'd actually, crazily, fallen in love with, but it was not an everyday car. It wasn't something Lacy was going to sell, so what was she thinking?

For some reason that caddy had a way about it. And as she sat down in it, she felt her grams, one on each shoulder saying, "Drive, Izzy, drive." And as torn up, confused, and flustered as she was, she laughed—a much needed laugh—then did exactly as instructed.

She drove. Smiling all the way, even as tears filled her eyes.

Drive, baby, drive. Wow, how crazy was that?

So, what did she do? She drove across the countryside until she drove into Stephenville, Texas, the closest town that actually had shopping, and that's what she did. Shopping. She wasn't a shopper, but it was her day off and she wasn't ready to head back to Mule Hollow. Still, she loved jeans, T-shirts, and flip-flops or tennis shoes. She wasn't normally a shopper.

But today she was. Anything to keep her away from her house on the same road as Luc lived on. So, shop she did—but didn't buy anything.

Three hours later, she finally headed out of

Stephenville—passing by the Cowboy Capital Walk of Fame in the downtown area, which she found interesting but didn't have the time or urge to go check it out. Instead, she headed back toward Mule Hollow through the country roads that had linked all these tiny, many now dead, towns around here. Like Mule Hollow, their huge, early oil boom had set them on the map but then most of it collapsed and the towns died...they didn't have the Mule Hollow matchmakers to get the idea to bring women to town to marry the cowboys that worked long hours and didn't have time to travel all the way to a large enough town to maybe find a date.

And that was how the Mule Hollow *Wives Wanted Campaign* had been born, by the dream of Esther Mae, Norma Sue, and Adela, and they'd brought Lacy Brown and Sheri Marsh to town in this pink caddy, and the party had begun.

It was a story of success and fascinated many. Her grams being the biggest fans, so here she was living there and in trouble. As she reached the edge of Stephenville, she saw a used car business, but it wasn't the sign that caught her gaze, it was the sparkly pale green, almost mint-toned convertible sitting on a ramp beneath the sign. It was a pretty two-seater, and unable to help herself, she yanked the steering wheel and whipped the big caddy into the drive.

What are you doing?

She parked the car near the other car that she thought was a T-bird. A design they'd come out with for a few short years, maybe four, then halted the sales, but she saw them around and they'd always got her attention.

What are you doing?

She walked up the small hill the car sat on, not a ramp but an actual low-lying hill made for the car to sit on and show it off. It worked because it had caught her attention.

It was not the usual colors she'd seen on other cars, the bright red, soft yellow, black, and a blue one. Those she'd seen but this was a sparkling light mint tone, and it drew her. The interior was soft leather and drew her as well. But it was not new—

"It's a 2003 model," a man said, walking up the small hill to stand across from her on the passenger's side. "Open the door and sit down. These only came out for four years, then they stopped. This particular one is a special edition, and only twelve hundred were produced with a soft bright color. It's got the engine of a Jaguar and sails—if you like that sort of thing. If you don't, it's an easy ride fast or slow. Want to test it out?"

She had sat down in the seat when he'd suggested it, unable not to. And now her hands were on the steering wheel, and she just sat there. It was much, much smaller than the pink Cadillac but that was fine, it was just her. It had an engine—he'd said of a Jaguar.

"You're saying it has speed and sails like the wind?"

He grinned and leaned on the door to point to the speedometer. It said 160 on it. "It'll do what you want or are comfortable doing. Hopefully not that."

She grinned. "I sometimes feel like I'm going that fast. My brain doesn't slow down like I want it to, but driving that fast, no, I don't think so."

And so, she'd let that be her reason for getting back in the caddy and heading home to Mule Hollow.

She'd started her morning early and it was only one

o'clock when she drove into Mule Hollow—too early to go home and chance running into the man down the street. So, she went to check out the clothing store her grams had told her about since the owner had been a match made in Mule Hollow.

She almost laughed, who wasn't a match made in Mule Hollow?

Me.

She parked the caddy in front of the store and walked inside. Instantly the charming, packed store impressed her and had her wondering why in the world she'd driven all the way to Stephenville after checking on her car. Ashby's Treasures had everything.

"*You* are Izzy Cranberry," a beautiful lady said as she came from behind the counter with her hand held out. "I'd heard you were moving to town. Thanks for coming in. I'd have been at your welcoming but was out of town. I'm Ashby."

"It's no big deal. And I'm glad to meet you. This is an amazing store."

She smiled. "Thank you. I work really hard to be creative and hit all the different types of ladies who come to Mule Hollow. How can I help you?"

"I'm really not a shopper. Just a jeans and T-shirt gal, but I'm new in town and thought I'd check things out instead of hanging out at the house."

Ashby grinned. "I've felt that before. I remember when I came to town, I was used to the big city but had an online store so thought a change would be good and this place drew me. And once I got here I never left. But believe me, God had a plan. I opened this store, and I have supplied everything for ladies when they come in. I have a small selection of cowboy boots, wedding dresses—have a wonderful area for that—jeans and an assortment of dress clothes for special occasions or dates." She smiled. "In Mule Hollow, that is sometimes a must have."

"It looks great." It was true there was a great array of styles and Izzy was drawn to the dresses—why, she wasn't sure, but they were so pretty. Soft colors, different lengths and styles. "As odd as it sounds, we all have a destiny. Not everyone figures it out, but for me, it's my dress store and moving here and helping find clothes for ladies and listening to them. Lacy found her calling in hair and here in town helping the matchmakers and just being there for anyone who needs her. And I've heard yours is similar.

"Looking in those eyes of yours, I see a very caring person and you can listen and keep things to yourself. I can too, and that's important. Giving people a place to talk is a calling people don't always realize is needed, but it's important."

She smiled, feeling a connection to Ashby as her words flowed out to her. "That's the way I look at it too."

Ashby's expression grew concerned. "I know we just met, and you don't have to trust me, but is something bothering you today? I'm here and would like to help or just get to know you. But no matter what, I'm here and would love to help you shop or give you quiet time to shop alone if that's what you need."

She was awesome. Even though Izzy was tempted because her heart was so heavy, she just smiled and then walked over to the dresses that hung on the rack. "These are beautiful. I...I'm not one to talk a lot, I listen. That's what I do. But I can see that you see things, and I want to say thanks for the offer. But I also have this strong, strange desire to buy a beautiful dress. One of these casual but beautiful ones to dress up or down."

"You have a great eye. That's exactly what they are. I'm not saying this is why you're looking, but they are perfect for a date. And that is one thing I always think about when I go to market, picking out things for my store. Ladies come here to catch the eye of a cowboy. And I'm here to help." She smiled. "I love it. I smile and hope they know through my smile and actions that I love the Lord and He's been good to me by bringing me here, showing me my sweet, amazing Dan and giving me the love of helping other ladies find the perfect outfit that's going to make a cowboy sit up and take notice. And maybe fall in love. A maybe because me and my clothes are not responsible for that. The gal, the cowboy, and God, that's who is responsible for that—so we are just going to look at these dresses and you try on all you want to. You don't have to buy anything."

Izzy's gaze stuck on the dress that was a soft gold that merged into a soft orange and deepened at the hem to almost rust. The combination was... "This is like a sunrise—no, a sunset."

"On target. I call it my sunrise-sunset dress. I couldn't pass it up when I saw it. I love the sunrise in the morning when you wake up early and peek out the window and see just that combination on the horizon. It's a romantic look and called to me at the market. Is it calling to you?"

Izzy couldn't deny it. "Very much so." She reached for the dress, found her size, then Ashby led her to the dressing room.

"You put it on, and I've got a pair of shoes to show you."

Izzy quickly changed, and her heart clenched when she saw herself in the mirror. She couldn't pass it up and knew that one day, not anytime soon, but one day she would wear this dress on her first real date, looking for her future.

One thing she wasn't ever going to start was dating casually. She just didn't have the time or the desire. She would be alert and watchful and shut things down the minute it didn't feel right. It didn't mean she was going to know right away, but she'd be on the lookout. She'd made a mistake and gone out with a young man early on who was a deceptive con artist. She figured out that he had his eye on getting her inheritance from her grams and also trying to teach her to be manipulated by him. She, thank goodness, saw through him and tossed him over the cliff of no return. Thank goodness her strong grams had rubbed off on her and she'd seen through him. She hated thinking about who ended up with him, but then learned one day that he'd married. She'd smartened up when he'd had an affair though and set herself free.

The young woman probably had an eye like Izzy's after that, an eye for seeing jerks quickly. At least that was what Izzy called it, but she was also a standoffish gal after that and didn't get approached often.

Fine with her. She had her plans and would be on track soon. After fulfilling her grams' dream of checking out this great town.

Thankfully, that one wrong move of dating a jerk had taught her also that when she did start looking for love, it would be with very penetrating eyes looking for anything that could be wrong. And it would be on her timing and no one else's.

But this dress. There was a knock on the door, and she realized she'd been staring at herself in the mirror for several minutes.

"I have a pair of shoes I couldn't resist ordering when I picked out the dress."

Izzy opened the door and stared at the pale beige heels that were beautiful. Not too tall and not too low. Instantly Izzy sat down on the stool by the door and slipped the shoes on her bare feet. "They fit perfectly. And I love them." She stood, stunned by how perfect she felt in this outfit. She smiled at Ashby, and said, "You are awesome. I'll take both the dress and the shoes and…I'll have to try that dress there on too." And so that was the way she spent the next thirty minutes. Trying on clothes and enjoying herself with Ashby.

And happily, not thinking about the cowboy who lived next door to her.

Well, almost not thinking of him.

CHAPTER NINETEEN

Luc stayed away from town all week until Thursday when he had to go pick up feed at Pete's feed store. So, he headed out after nine o'clock because he knew Heavenly Inspirations opened at nine and his neighbor was always on time. He'd ridden the ranch riding one of his freshly broken horses that needed a good ride out in the open. Knowing she was at work, he'd let himself ride across the pastures and up the hill that overlooked the little house with the sparkling wind chimes singing in the breeze.

He'd sat there, and despite not wanting to, he'd looked at that small back porch and wondered what it would be like to sit there with her on a starlit night with the fireflies sparkling about them, the wind chimes sounding softly and the scent of honeysuckles filling the breeze.

Why that ran through his brain, he wasn't sure—that porch looked inviting. He had a porch—and sat on it alone and watched the night pass by, but lately the hours seemed to stretch on endlessly and silently.

He turned then and rode the horse away and didn't plan on going back. No need messing up his brain any more than it already was. He'd made a decision not to talk to her again because he'd almost opened up to her. Pace had said that sometimes talking helped ease the heart. And his had eased up some over the years, but ever since she'd arrived, nothing had eased up. It had only intensified.

He wasn't sleeping, he wasn't dreaming—because he wasn't sleeping—and that was good. Odd thing to not want, but the last thing he needed was to dream about the lady next door.

Dreaming about Izzy Cranberry wouldn't be good. It would have him wanting things he didn't want to want. Needing things he didn't want to need. Longing for love...

Man, he was in trouble.

When you love, you lose, and he couldn't go there—but today he had to go to Pete's Feed and Seed and there was no way around it. So, he'd head in, get what he needed, then come back home.

That was the easy situation. Tomorrow there was no avoidance because he had to go to a party at Norma Sue and Roy Don's house. And Izzy would be there.

He drove into town past the pink salon to the yellow feed store and pulled into a parking space in front and headed inside. Only then did he see that App and Stanley were standing at the counter with Pete.

Today they were buying a new five-pound bag of sunflower seeds. They didn't use tobacco but always had a spittoon in the diner that they spit their sunflower shells into when they were through grinding them through their teeth. He'd played with them several times and the ping happened often when the shells flew out and pinged against the wide metal entrance to the spittoon.

"Hey, fellas, is it sunflower seed refill time?"

App was the first to speak, even though he was supposed to be the hardest of hearing. "Yep, can't play checkers all day long without spitting a few shells into the pot and hearing it zing."

"Well, that's what we've gotten used to," Stanley said with a big wide grin. "Pete's having to find us giant seeds these days so the zing will be loud enough for us to hear."

"And we like the taste of them too," Applegate broke in. "Sam lets us do it, so what the heck. Hey, you need to come play checkers with us today."

"Well, I actually came in to see Pete. I need horse feed, then I'm heading back to the house."

Applegate put a really thin fist on his thin hip, his brows dipped making his sour expression even more intense. "You tryin' to avoid that pretty hairdresser, Izzy?"

"No, where did you get that idea?"

"There's no reason to deny it. That one day we saw interest in your eyes and you ain't had that look for any other woman who has passed your way since you've been here. And then there was the pig incident. Believe me, we've been watching."

His gaze went to Pete. "Don't ask me to jump in."

Right. This wasn't something many people wanted to jump into other than Norma Sue, Esther Mae, and Adela. "Look, I know y'all sit in there and pretend you can't hear, but everyone in town knows you turn those superpowered hearing aids on and can hear everything that goes on in that place. Or any place. So, did you two hear something I need to know?"

They looked at each other then back at him.

"Well," Stanley said. "We did hear the ladies talking yesterday. They have decided that since Lacy put Izzy out there at that house where she and Sheri first lived when they moved to town, that maybe she knows something about you and Izzy that everybody else doesn't know. Whether it's true or not, we don't know. Nor do the three matchmaking schemers, but we do know she's a great hairdresser. That is all we've heard, and I have to tell you that everyone is talking about what a great hairdresser she is, like Lacy. And well, they think because her grams sent her here that maybe there's a reason."

"What does that have to do with me?"

Applegate slapped his hand on his thigh. "You do

207

live in the house where Pace lived, and you did come here from the same place Pace came from. You know, the lonesome, vast area of nowhere land. Where nobody is around, especially in the winter, but you and the cattle you're taking care of. Means you're a loner or a hider. And even though Pace is a fella that keeps his mouth shut, we're all coming to the conclusion that he got you here for a reason—a good reason."

"That you need help," Pete said, then grimaced because he'd added to the conversation.

App hitched a brow. "And whether you think me and Stanley are matchmakers or not, we are good helpers. I may look like a grouchy old toothpick, but if God puts somebody in front of me, my quizzical brain starts working. And it's been workin'."

"Believe me," Stanley grunted. "It's been workin'. This dude gets something on his mind, and he doesn't stop thinkin' about it. And he has *you* on his mind, you, checker player. 'Cause we know when you play checkers it's a relief to your overworked mind. That mind that doesn't always show itself. But you sing in the choir, and we see your face, and we know without a doubt that something hard is biting at you. There is something going on in that brain of yours underneath that cowboy hat, and we got a feelin' that the Lord is workin'."

He just stared at the usually short-spoken men...what? What was going on?

"Pete, I need some feed. I need it in my truck, and I need it now. I'll go load it myself for that matter." He sucked in a breath. "Guys, there is nothing going on. Nothing I want to talk about, even if there was something going on, so you can all back off because I am not your next mission."

With that, he handed Pete his list and headed to the back. Pete had already pushed the door open. They both walked into the big, wide feed storage area. There were huge stacks of feed and seed and anything else you needed on a ranch. There was an area you could pull your truck up in the back and get big loads or have them delivered, but he wasn't getting that big a load.

He'd parked in front—it slammed into him then that from where he'd parked, he could see Heavenly Inspirations, Sam's Diner, Pete's Feed and Seed, and the

Prickly Pear Jelly Store. From where he was parked, he could see every entrance and everyone and *anyone* who parked or walked in and out of those stores.

Why had he parked there? Why had he not pulled in back to load his truck there?

He knew the answer. He was in denial, but he wasn't going to see her.

"Come on over and play checkers with us. It's been a few days."

At App's statement, Luc spun around and there stood the two schemers staring at him with their big bag of sunflower seeds held in App's skinny arms.

"Guys, lay off. Just stop this."

"Look," Applegate drawled. "We will shut up, but you got a stressed look on your face and sometimes checkers helps."

"And if that don't help," Stanley added. "Sam's coffee or dessert will help."

They just stared at him, and he sighed. They were trying to help him. "Look, guys, I don't know what to think right now. But I'm not looking to be one of the matches made in Mule Hollow. I didn't come here for that. Yeah, I'll be truthful to you two and you too, Pete. I came here because Pace knew I needed a place to start over. A place to not be hidden. He knew that I wasn't a loner and that Mule Hollow would be a good place for me to be—but not to be made a match. So, I do enjoy playing checkers with y'all. When I was alone out there in the winters by myself, I played checkers with myself. I played one side and then the other. It was ridiculous, so yes, you guys, I enjoy being around y'all and it has nothing to do with being matchmade."

All three grinned. The wrinkles on App's face were everywhere, the not seen much smile crinkled everything like he'd never seen. And Stanley's eyes brightened, and he smiled from one ear to the other, reminding him of Norma Sue's wide smile that practically wrapped around both ears. That lady had the biggest smile he'd ever seen. And Pete, well, he was grinning a gotcha grin that spoke volumes.

"Alright, I'll come play a game of checkers with y'all, but I might not stay long."

Pete picked up the bag of feed and walked past him toward the door. "Good decision. Sometimes you just need to step outside your limitations. I know I don't say a lot, but dude, you got boundaries like I've never seen before. So go on, I'll load these up while you go play checkers."

And so, there he was walking down the wooden sidewalk toward Sam's Diner, and when they got close, he saw Norma Sue come out of the diner. Then she headed toward Heavenly Inspirations with a grin on her face.

CHAPTER TWENTY

Izzy was working and Lacy was off today and tomorrow and was also taking the rest of the week off.

Izzy was finishing up on Pollyanna Talbert's hair when Norma Sue came into the salon.

"I'm supposed to get my hair done, but I feel like eating, so let's put my hair off and head over and eat some lunch," Norma Sue said the moment she came inside.

Izzy was supposed to do her hair today and now it slammed into her that maybe Norma Sue didn't want her doing her hair after she'd seen her do Esther Mae's. "Norma, if you don't want me to do your hair, it's okay."

"No, no, I do want you to do it, but I'm starving, and you know when I'm hungry I sometimes get dizzy—well, not too bad. I just want some food. Come on, my treat. All of y'all. Esther Mae and Adela are already over there with the table."

She'd just finished cutting Pollyanna's hair, a really small lady with long curly hair who ran a bed-and-breakfast outside of town beside her and her husband's ranch. It sounded fun. The song "Old McDonald" had come to life with the four children they had and the animals she'd told her about—a singing cockatiel, goats, and they were now raising the shar-pei breed of dogs because of their dog Bogie, who was aging, and they wanted to carry his fun spirit with them always bred into his puppies. Very sweet since Pollyanna had lost her first husband and Bogie had helped them through the loss.

Izzy wondered if Luc needed one of the puppies—*stop*. She was not letting her mind go to her neighbor, who kept refusing to get out of her mind.

"It sounds like fun," Pollyanna said as she picked up her purse. "But I have to get back to my B&B. Guests are coming for the night and I need to be there before they think my cockatiel talking to them through the door in my voice is really me." She grinned. "We never know what he's going to say. Once they know about him, they love his surprising words, but to start off with, I need to be there. I love my hair, and I also have to cook for the evening meal. But I have to say that I think what's cooking over at the diner sounds good."

She looked at Norma Sue. "You know I'm always grateful for y'all's cooking and looking forward to the party tomorrow night. Y'all can tell me then how lunch goes. I know Sam's is a great place to get great cooking too."

Why did all this conversation about cooking sound a little odd? She'd already paid Izzy and before she left, Pollyanna patted her on the arm. "Enjoy lunch, and I can promise you these ladies in town can be very entertaining at lunch."

And then she walked out the door and left Izzy standing there with a forty-five-minute appointment and lunch break combined. And she couldn't exactly say no. "Okay, lead the way."

Lacy had warned her that sometimes sporadic things happened and the best thing to do was just go along with them. She hadn't been exactly sure whether to take that seriously or not. Now, she was even more worried about how to take it. She followed the grinning Norma Sue out the door, locked it, then they crossed the road and entered Sam's Diner. It was lunchtime and folks filled the place. Sam was talking to the checker players and blocking the view of the cowboy at the table with them. Esther Mae and Adela were at the table right behind him, and when they saw her, they smiled big and waved her over, giving her a great welcome.

She tried to relax the sudden tension filling her, this was good. They were accepting her and making her a part of their party...so why, oh, why did it seem a little off?

She sat down in the chair Esther Mae was patting. It was the chair facing Sam's back, and Norma Sue sat down in the chair beside her since Adela was sitting in the chair closest to her husband's back. Something was odd...but what?

Then in the next instant Sam turned her direction

with a grin on his face as he placed his wrinkled hand on his wife's shoulder and gave her a sweet, soft pat. "Hey, ladies, it's good to see you. And Izzy, it's lunchtime, and I see you have a great view." Then he stepped to the side and the man who was sitting in the chair facing the window was none other than her neighbor.

As she was realizing the setup, he glanced at her, and she saw he'd realized they were being set up too. Now, they were looking eye to eye.

"Looky who else is here," Esther Mae cooed. "I didn't see you since Sam was standing in my line of vision. All our lines of vision. So, how do you like playing checkers with those two conniving little dudes?"

"Don't be saying bad things about us," Applegate barked. "You know you have your bad side or *sides* too."

"I'm just teasing," Esther Mae cooed. "Y'all know I enjoy y'all's awful ways, especially right now because y'all have a *good* cowboy sitting with you. He's probably about to teach you two how to really play checkers."

Throughout the conversation, she and Luc were staring at each other. She had a feeling they'd both been manipulated into this because he looked as shocked as she felt.

"Well, now come on, everyone," Adela said softly. "It's going to be a great meal. Sam, will you please bring me my coffee? Ladies, what would you like? You three enjoy your game, we're going to have a meal and enjoy ourselves."

So, Adela's part in this was to calm the plot down.

It was time to go. He needed to, but despite everything, he'd been listening to the conversation at the table behind him. Izzy had said, when asked loudly by Norma Sue if she'd ridden a horse yet, that no, not yet. And that maybe she wouldn't before she left.

She was leaving. His mind hadn't been on the games but on the conversation. This game was with Stanley, and he'd made his play and then Stanley made his and took him out.

"Well, I gotcha and don't feel good about it because you haven't been concentrating. You know you're a better player than that. It was as easy as tic-tac-toe."

"Yeah, guys, I've got to go. Thanks. It was, as always, nice being here with you two, and let's just say I'm about to make y'all's day. Don't know if her answer is going to make your day but my question is." He stood up, turned and, because his words had purposely been loud enough for the cowboys to hear, all four ladies sitting at the table behind him were looking at him. Even Izzy.

"Was that about me?" she asked, being direct.

"Yes, actually. I realized when I heard you say you hadn't ridden a horse yet that I had told you I would take you riding, and I haven't. Well, today is a great day for it, so if you have time when you get off, then I would be happy to take you." He was fumbling his sentences. "Look, I'm going home, I have a great horse for you, and I'll saddle him, and he'll be waiting there today. No pressure. You show, and we'll ride. I'll make sure you're safe, and I'll make sure Mammoth isn't around." He took his hat off. "Ladies, y'all have a great day."

He saw that Izzy was in shock as he turned and left them all sitting there, reached the door, caught Sam watching him from a table of customers near the door that he was waiting on. Sam gave him a thumbs up that Izzy couldn't see.

Had he been that loud so the whole diner had heard? Had everyone heard him ask her to ride horses with him? He walked on out the door—what would be would be and that was all there was to it.

He got home and did exactly what he said he would. He picked the pretty, very tame horse, one of Pace's horses that belonged to his wife, Sheri. Because, like Izzy, Sheri hadn't been a cowgirl when she'd moved here. She'd been a manicurist. She'd married a horse trainer and breaker like him. So, he walked the tame mare out and tied her to the fence so if Izzy drove that pink caddy into the yard, she'd see Goldie and know he'd been telling the truth.

And then, to get his mind off the lady he wanted to come ride horses with him really badly, he headed for the stable where the not tame horses waited their turn. He opened the back gate and let one of the horses into the backyard, then he opened the alley gate that the horse would take and end up in his arena. Within moments he was in the arena with a wild stallion.

It was a good way to get a calm brain when a stallion wanted a fight. It took a calm brain, calculating and consistent to tame him down. So, Luc needed a wild horse right now to help calm his insanity down.

Why had he invited her to ride?

The ladies had instantly urged her to take him up on his offer.

Because her grams would want her to ride a horse with a cowboy while she was in Mule Hollow. Even if she was going to pack up and leave later on, riding with a cowboy was an unforgettable time. And so, what did she do?

She used it as an excuse to drive this pink caddy past her house. It was now almost four o'clock, and she ended up at Luc's.

The first thing she spotted was the beautiful golden-toned horse with the pale mane. It was gorgeous and waiting for her tied to a fence. She didn't have to wonder where he was, she knew. He wasn't waiting on her, he'd just done what he said and readied a horse for her. He'd known she'd come—or *hoped* she'd come.

She didn't need to be thinking that. She didn't need to wonder if he was hoping something would happen between them. It wasn't a good thought for her. But she certainly didn't want him wondering the same thing. They were just two people caught up in the wrong thing. The thing that neither of them wanted, especially him—she shut all thoughts down.

Shut them down.

Her heart wasn't connected to this. To him.

They were just going to ride a horse.

A song kept coming into her brain, she couldn't remember the song, couldn't recall the name, but she just knew that in the song somebody was riding a horse. Were they riding across a pasture, were they riding across a street, were they riding a horse together?

She and Luc were going to be riding separate horses—no riding a horse together. She looked at that horse again, was it a tame horse? No chance of her getting bucked off since this was her very first horse ride ever. As she studied it, she got out of her car and the horse moved, turned toward her and nickered in a very kind, soft way. Flicked its head to the side and almost looked like it smiled at her.

Oh, yeah, this was a nice horse. No way a horse looking at her like that could be a bad horse.

And whether she wanted to or not, she trusted Luc to have lined up a very tame horse for her to ride.

She walked toward the arena that was toward the back where she'd seen him before. She reached it, and there he was inside that arena with a horse that wasn't happy. The moment she walked up, the horse was reared up on his long back legs clawing his two front hooves at Luc. Luc had his pole with the flag at the top and calmly stood there unmoved as he waved it to the side of the angry horse. He held the reins as the horse continued his show of anger.

Luc could easily be hurt, stomped, trampled—but in her heart of hearts she knew that wouldn't happen. Luc could handle anything a horse wanted to throw at him. He waved the flag. The horse dropped to all four hooves and stared at Luc, clearly trying to determine what his next move would be. Probably wondering why, with all of his raging, the cowboy was still as calm as could be. But clearly the ornery horse was trying to figure out its next move.

Like her. Was she ornery? Yep. Her grams sang together. *Yep,   yep,   yep,   you're ornery...cantankerous...just being plain grouchy—*

"Gee, now Grams are making up songs about me inside my own head," she muttered softly then took a breath and made herself known. "I'm here," she said loud enough for him but hopefully not loud enough to irritate the horse more.

Instantly Luc turned her way. "Awesome, I'm here too."

The two of them, going on a ride...

CHAPTER TWENTY-ONE

He had worked with the horse for maybe forty minutes and the horse wasn't happy. It didn't matter though because the moment he heard Izzy's voice he was out of there. And he knew he was in trouble. He'd been going through his brain all of this time instead of concentrating on the horse. Why had he asked her to come out today? He knew he'd had to.

Yeah, when this was all over, they'd go their separate ways, but right now all he wanted to do was take her on a horse ride through this beautiful country. Show her something she wanted to see, wanted to know about, and he wanted to be the one to show her everything her grams wanted her to see.

Everything else rolling through his brain, he pushed

back into a separate slot and slammed the lock on it. He'd deal with it later, but today, this afternoon, he was a free man, not thinking about his past or his future. All he was thinking about was taking this beautiful, kind woman on a ride she'd never forget.

A ride that would make her grams happy.

"I'm glad you came. Goldie is out there waiting, and I can promise you she's a great horse. Pace trained her, and she's the second horse he trained for his wife, Sheri. She'd come to Mule Hollow and never ridden a horse before either. She'd ridden in that pink caddy and came to town to watch her friend work magic—" He chuckled at the thought. "Anyway, Lacy isn't the only lady you have something in common with, you also have Sheri's drive. She was Lacy's friend and rode along to watch the party start. Like you came along to let your grams ride along with you."

She smiled at his words. "They are and that's for certain."

His heart dipped like a skydiver enjoying his jump. "We're going to give your grams a great day. Just forget about everything else. That's what I'm going to do. I'm not going to marry, and you're not going to stay. Let's just say today we're going to make everyone in your mind and up in heaven happy. Even those gals at the diner and App, Stanley, and Sam too. We're just going to make them all glad today, they just won't know it's not going anywhere further."

She smiled. "We have a deal."

Then she held her hand out for a shake. He held his out, then their hands locked together as if meant to be. Electric sensation shot through him like he'd just grabbed hold of an electric fence. He looked to the ground not wanting her to see his reaction because it was so strong there was no way his expression wasn't lit up. Then he had to look at her and there was a shock to her eyes that told him she'd either had the same sensation as he'd had, or she was horrified by the touch. He let go then, had to because if he didn't, he might pull her into his arms and kiss her and pray that look in her eyes was the same amazing feeling racing through him even now.

Where was his mind going?

This was a horse ride and making her grams happy.

That other stuff, the good stuff, needed to go.

He turned toward the horse, but she continued to just stand there. He had to give her a moment, and he had to focus on the horse and get a grip on his head—his heart. He had to pray he didn't swing around and take her in his arms.

Give up the arms already. You're not holding her today.

Or ever.

You're not going to kiss her.

She didn't want it and he didn't either.

"Okay, I've got her ready, but I'm going to leave her tied up." He took a deep breath and put his hand on the horse's forehead and ran it down to her nose. "If you'll step over here, you can pet Goldie while I go get my horse."

While I go in and calm down and you stay out here and calm down if you're having similar reactions to something neither of us wants.

She stepped up beside him, didn't look at him but placed her hand beside his but didn't touch it. She watched as he ran his hand down the horse's forehead.

Then she did the same, ran her hand down the white streak running from Goldie's forehead to her nose—was her hand trembling?

"Good job. You two stand here and get to know each other, and I'll be back." And then he walked away, striding across the dirt to the stables.

Izzy almost lost her mind as she did what he told her, petted the horse and tried to calm down. That handshake—oh, goodness she'd almost passed out. In her brain, she'd wanted him to kiss her.

To sweep her into his arms, off her feet, and kiss her. She'd never looked at a man and thought that until Luc. Well, maybe as a teen but never anything that compared to the moment seconds before. *Get your brain on straight, cowgirl*—cowgirl. That was the last thing she was. What was she thinking? She wasn't going to be here long enough to even think about becoming one either.

Thankfully, here he came striding out of that barn. Leading that horse, that big, tall horse. It was as broad-shouldered as he was—for a horse and a man they matched up well.

What? Yep, she'd lost her mind.

The horse was a bronze tone, like a trophy, and Luc was going to be with his match one day—*not that I'm going to try for that position.*

No, they were just going on a ride to make her grams have a great day—okay, so they were in heaven and always having a great day. But she was not taking it back or changing it to her having a great day. This was all for them.

She was just getting a moment, an afternoon, to relax and him too. That was all this was to her. And maybe he would talk…

"Your horse is beautiful. Can I call a stallion beautiful?"

He smiled—*goodness gracious, great smile of fire!* Yep, Jerry Lee Lewis was singing in her head again.

"You can call him whatever you want to call him. This is your day." His eyes danced and so did her insides. "Not sure what classifies a man for that—"

You.

"But he does pretty good with the mares."

Her brain was going crazy. "I can see why. Have you had him a long time or did you just break him?"

"I've had Racer for a long time. He came here with me from Idaho. He has a great easy temperament."

And so do you. It was true. The man was always in control, and she was going to have to learn from him.

"Now let's get you in the saddle. Do you trust me?"

"Yes, I do." There was no hesitation in her answer because it was true. She trusted this man like she'd never trusted anyone before. The thought struck her hard. "There's no denying that you know what you're doing, and I trust you, after all you already saved me from a rattlesnake and then pulled me from my wrecked car."

That smile of his spread across his handsome face again and spread through her internally like melting butter—sweet butter—honey butter—*shut up!*

"Then we're going to get this done. Come here."

"Okay, here we go." She moved to stand beside him, feeling the closeness and trying hard to ignore it.

"Now, I've got the reins; you can have them on the

next saddle up place this hand on the saddle horn then lift that foot and place it in the stirrup, those shoes will work just fine. Now, lift up with your leg putting all the pressure there as you pull with that hand on the saddle horn, then toss the other leg over the horse and slide into the saddle."

His voice was calm, steady and comforting, endearing—she ignored where her head was going as she did exactly as he'd instructed her to do. She put her casual, flat shoed foot in the stirrup, stood up and amazingly she settled into that saddle like she'd been born to do it.

"That was nowhere near as complicated as I thought it would be."

He grinned that amazing grin and his hand was still on the horse's neck, still holding the reins. Even though she was in the saddle, he was still in control, and she knew it. She just didn't need him to be in control of her. But, in that moment, who cared?

"Now, she is trained not to run off or anything, but let's say we are riding along and I've given you these reins and for some unknown reason she spooks and takes off running, these reins and that saddle horn have a reason, so grab hold of the horn and with your other hand pull hard toward you on these reins pulling her head back. And she'll slow down, and I'll be at your side by then. Do you trust me?"

Did she trust him? "Yes, I do."

I do.

The words rang through her sounding like she was standing at the wedding altar and the preacher had been saying, "Do you take this man as your—" *Whoa.*

Whoa, Izzy, back up. This was getting crazy. And her grams, she could hear them up in heaven hooting and hollering and having a good time.

Oh, my goodness. What was wrong with her— honestly at the moment she was on a horse. About to ride a horse, her grams were having a heavenly time and when she opened her eyes, she was looking into the gaze of a man who could stop any woman's heartbeat. Yes, she was going to have a good day.

And there was nothing that was going to stop her from having a great day. This possibly could be the best day of her life.

An odd thought, but she took it. When he turned and walked away from her, she knew that later when they got back, she'd be fine with that because she'd be walking away too.

But like he'd said, today was a free day and she wasn't going to give it up.

CHAPTER TWENTY-TWO

Hugging the saddle, she smiled wildly as she looked down at the cowboy standing beside her horse. Her heart was thundering not with just the excitement that this cowboy had a great idea, but with the fact she was having a great time, and she hadn't even taken the horse for its first step.

"So, now what?"

"Hold on to these reins, and I'll load up, and we'll head out. What do you think?"

"I think you had a great idea. My grams wanted this, but I really do want to ride a horse, and it's such a nice horse."

He grinned with that perfect grin of his. "A lot of people don't think they want to ride one but then get on the back of a horse and get addicted. Me, I started out on a horse. My dad loved horses more than country music and passed it on to me. I competed in the rodeos, and he rooted me on. But then I got interested in taming horses, and I saw a man tame a horse like I do now. I was driven to do the same as he did and went to several of his classes teaching people how to calm and tame a horse without any rough treatment, and it all fell into place. Then after dad died—" He hesitated. "Okay, do this, watch what I do, and let's ride. We're going out to a fantastic ranch, and I know why Pace bought this ranch. There is a stream that winds through the land, then spreads out into a big lake. We're heading that way, and we can take a break. The stream and the lake make me think how much kids would love it—" No kids, why was he starting to talk about things he didn't want to talk about?

Yes, if he had a family, it would be an awesome place to spend family time. But he didn't and wasn't having a family. What was it about being around this woman that made his mind go where it had no business going and where he didn't want it to go?

He rode looking straight ahead and fought to get his brain where it was supposed to be. He'd told her they were going to have a good time. Not that he was going to ride in silence.

"You're right, it's beautiful," she said softly on the breeze. He looked at her and her eyes searched his, as if she sensed he had more going on in his head. She probably didn't know it had to do with her and the way she affected him like no one else ever had.

"It is. This is why after I train a horse, I ride him out here. Like the day I found you with the rattler. It's a beautiful area with the yellow flowers and bluebonnets that'll be gone soon. It's colorful. Peaceful." He needed peace often. Now.

"You're right. I feel like I'm riding in a painting."

She looked like a painting. "We're going to follow it over that hill across the pasture, we're going to take it slow and then we'll reach the top and you'll see the lake. You doing okay?"

"Yes, this sweet horse is so calm I have no fear. She'd never do anything to hurt me."

"Normally, but still hold on and keep your focus.

You know odd things can happen. There's the tale about Samantha the donkey." She was staring at him. "She and Lilly were in the Christmas play. Lilly was riding on her back while pregnant, playing Mary, and Samantha was the donkey she rode on in the real story. Lilly sang a beautiful song, then Samantha's tail caught fire. Calm, never mean Samantha and her tail was on fire. That donkey kicked and raced like she normally didn't do. Thank goodness Lilly knows how to ride and stayed on and then she was rescued by Cort—it was in one of Molly Popp's writeups and proves you never know when trouble is going to change everything—so stay alert."

Izzy was glad he'd already thought about that because she hadn't and for the first time she did. From the movement in the lower half of her body, she had a fear that something might be aching soon. And she'd been right.

But the ride was worth it. Bluebonnets mixed with a lot of yellow flowers running along the hillside. The cattle were further down the side of the direction they were going. Standing under the trees and some out in the sunshine. They were all munching on the grass and some calves were romping. It was peaceful...

Her mind went to Luc. Once again, he'd almost given her a glimpse of his past but realized it and gone instantly to talking about the lake. She was starting to become driven by the want to know what had happened to this man. But he did seem happier today and they'd made that truce that today was their day and then they'd walk away. She didn't let herself think about the gut wrench that struck her when those two words came into her thoughts...*walk away.*

Her plan was to walk away. Always had been, so why did her gut feel like it had been squeezed through a strainer?

Finally, they topped the hill. At last, she could stop thinking—she gasped at the sight of the large lake. She stared across it and the birds flying above them and the pastures and trees surrounding it. And the beautiful blue sky above it. "What a beautiful place."

"It is that."

She whispered, "I didn't even know I said that out loud. It was my brain talking."

Luc chuckled. "It was saying the right thing. Does it talk to you often?"

Yes, and sang to her too. But she did not say any of that out loud, thank goodness.

He grinned at her from where he sat in his saddle, his wrists crossed casually over the saddle horn as he watched her. He was so handsome but that wasn't what drew her. It was those eyes, sea-green eyes that were penetrating into her as they stared at each other.

"What?" she asked needing him to say why he was looking at her like that. Needing to know why she was reacting to him this way.

"I don't know, you're the first person I've ever shared this spot with. Pace built the pier out there and fastened the seats down so he didn't have to worry about anyone falling in if they sat down in them. So, you'll be safe when we sit on them. Come on, let's ride down this hill and sit for a while and talk."

It didn't take them long to reach the pier and before they even made it to a halt, he'd already dismounted in one swift motion.

And then stepped over to her and held his arms up then pulled them back as if realizing he was offering her a way off the horse without using her own muscles.

"Now let's see if you can get off like I showed you."

"Okay, here goes," she said, determined to do this right. She drew her leg over the back of the horse, holding her other foot in the stirrup and then when she went to lower herself to the ground, her foot slipped in the stirrup and she lost balance, but two large, firm hands wrapped around her waist and lifted her to the ground.

"I've got you, now you're standing up."

She was still facing the horse and Luc's hands were still holding each side of her waist. She had to thank him but...she turned. His hands eased up their hold but remained on her hips as she faced him. There was but an inch, maybe two, between them. Heart pounding, she met his gaze, his amazing sea-green eyes with the silver sparkle that surrounded the deep green more noticeable this close to him. Was he feeling what she felt?

"Thank you." Her palm came up and rested on his chest, his heart to be exact, as she felt the slamming of it against her palm.

His eyes suddenly sparked lightning as he breathed and in almost a whisper said, "This is foolish."

Her own heart thundering she stepped closer to him and then he bent his head, paused as their gazes locked and then they kissed.

It was as if they'd been on the same cue, then her knees wobbled, his hands tightened as if to steady her and his kiss was everything she'd ever dreamed of…yes, she'd dreamed of kisses and nothing had ever been close to reality.

Everything inside of her went on alarm as her knees got even weaker, his arms supported her as his lips told her he was feeling exactly what she was feeling.

And nothing, in that moment, mattered but the kiss and being in each other's arms—well, she was in his arms and hanging on. As his strong arms held her and his lips gave her everything she'd *never* ever dreamed of.

CHAPTER TWENTY-THREE

The woman in his arms was everything, her soft lips, her sweet gasp, her heart racing against his as she practically went limp in his arms. Telling him she felt the lightning too. Lightning on a dark night sky lighting everything up. Bringing with it the joy he never felt before.

This was what he feared more than anything else life could throw at him. He'd been dealt a terrible blow but now a kiss like this, that most looked at like a gift, was torment for him.

Having an overwhelming emotion inside of him for someone that he could never give in to was a harsh reality. He deepened his kiss out of desperation because he knew when he ended this kiss, never would he feel this again. His mind, his heart raced as the pain inside of him tried to steal the joy he felt. The amazing emotion he couldn't—if he ever lost her, the raging love inside of him that he knew he was feeling. That he feared he would feel as hard, harsh, and brutal.

He could never live through losing again, this was different, even deeper than losing his family. His kiss deepened, his embrace tightened, and he picked her off her feet as her arms slid around his neck and her fingertips slid into his short hair at the nape of his neck. She clung to him and him to her, even as his heart tore up inside.

He knew he would never, ever feel love like this again. He also knew that if he opened his heart and he lost her, it would be harder than anything. Even harder than losing the three people he loved the most in this world all at the same time, the same instant. The same hard impact that only he had woken up from alive.

He'd lost them all at one time. He felt the moisture in his eyes, and he had to let go. He could not let himself feel anything deeper than this.

Get control.

Get.

Control.

Now.

He'd brought her out here to give her a good day. He couldn't let her know…he eased up on the embrace, ended the kiss as her feet settled back on the ground. "I have to stop…we have to stop."

Her hands had slid from his hair and now down his chest to her side. Her expression was as shocked as he was certain his was also. He held her waist just to make sure she was steady and then she backed away.

"Yes, I didn't mean to do that."

"I didn't either. So…" He sucked in a breath. "Let's move out there on the open water. To the chairs that are attached to the pier and are safe to sit in."

"Right, let's do that." And she turned and led the way through the low growth of grass. She strode to the second chair as if wanting to get as far away from him as possible. He sank into the other chair not sure why he'd crossed that line and kissed her. Backtracking was going to be unbelievably hard.

Especially since now, she wasn't staring at him but at the water and she wasn't speaking. "I didn't mean to do that," he repeated.

She sighed and raked a hand through her hair. "I actually encouraged that, so I take the blame too. Luc, I am going to ask you what happened to you. I know that you have no plans for a woman, and I have no plans for a man here in Mule Hollow. But I think I scared you though. So, tell me, Luc Asher, what happened to you?"

He stared at her. "I told you not to ask me." She hitched a brow of challenge. "Fine. I was driving a car. My dad's car. My dad and mom and my sister. We were going to the park where we were going to celebrate my mom's birthday—" His throat tightened. "I was driving because Dad had twisted his ankle working in the yard. We were almost there on the freeway when a drunk driver drove his car onto the freeway going the wrong way. I didn't see it until the big moving truck in front of me swerved out of its way, leaving me just a second and not enough time to react before the drunk slammed into us at a high speed."

Izzy's hand slammed to her heart, he continued. "In an instant, everything changed. I didn't even have time to yank the steering wheel either way before he slammed into us. Before we were slammed into by the drunk, who didn't even realize he was going the wrong way until it was too late." His voice trembled.

"I'm so very sorry. I don't even know what to say."

"Exactly why I don't talk about it."

Her expression had changed from horror to a gentle compassion that was clear. "It wasn't your fault, Luc. You can't blame yourself. How long ago was this?"

"Ten years. Ten long, drawn-out years."

Ten years. "I'm so very sorry." What else could she say?

Her heart hurt for him but something inside her pushed her to say more. "So, you live your life afraid." *What?* That hadn't been what she'd meant to say.

He stood up and strode to the edge of the planks, put his hands on his hips, his shoulders stiff as he stared out at the water, his back to her. "I guess you could call it that," he finally said, turning to look at her. "I call it control."

Staring up at him she suddenly wanted to throw herself at him, hug him—*punch him in the stomach.* Her thoughts about him were all knotted up. Needing to get herself under control, she stood too. "This place might be beautiful, but I need to get back home."

She started walking away, it was either that or do another, even crazier thing than kiss the man.

He didn't say anything, just followed her. At the horses, the calm, grass-nibbling horses, she took the reins, prayed she mounted the horse without incident and then, without waiting, she rode back the way they'd come.

What a day this had been. Like a wild, out-of-control roller coaster that she wasn't sure how to react to. All she knew for certain was it was time to put space between them. When they reached the stable, he was off his horse instantly and she was too, thank goodness.

"Thanks for the ride. Now, I'm heading home." And she did. Not peacefully. And not with her grams singing in her head. Those two had somehow gone silent.

CHAPTER TWENTY-FOUR

The party was well underway by the time Izzy talked herself into going and entered Norma Sue's backyard. She'd almost not come because she knew Luc was going to be here. If he hadn't wanted to come because of her, he would come anyway because this wasn't about them. This was a town gathering.

"Hey, there, good to see you again, Izzy."

She smiled at tiny Pollyanna as she walked up. "Hey, good to see you here."

"I have to tell you that I love my hair. It's just a little shorter, but the fullness of the cut is fun. My son likes it too. He'll probably come in and get his cut soon. He has curl too and when you meet him, you'll remember him. Sixteen is an adventurous age, and he is trying to live up to it. My husband liked it too."

"I'm so glad."

"So, are you here to dance? If so, who do you have your eyes on?"

"No, I'm not here to dance and have my eyes on no one."

"Most of the ladies don't when they first arrive in town. I didn't. I wasn't looking for love again. I'd already had a wonderful man and lost him. I had no, absolutely no plans to live through loving a man with all my heart and then losing him ever again. Grief is hard. But God worked in wonderful ways in my life. And my sweet son's life and my husband's life."

"I know He works in everyone's life, but your words seem deep."

"Yes, I lost my first husband, Marc, and he was wonderful. We'd already decided to move to a small town, so I did it. I had no plans to ever remarry because I didn't think I could ever be that happy again…" Her voice trembled.

"I'm sorry, I didn't mean to upset you." She was remarried and still emotional about her first marriage.

How could that be? She seemed so happy.

Pollyanna smiled. "Oh, no, Marc has been dead for several years and I thought I could never have that kind of happiness again. I moved here to bring up my son and my last name was McDonald so "Old McDonald" was on my mind." She smiled and so did Izzy as the song played in her mind. "I took on a lot of responsibilities just to keep myself occupied. I had to move forward. Same with Nate next door on his ranch. He'd had a wonderful life with his beloved first wife and knew no one could replace her. And he was right, we both were right. We learned our hearts can open wide, and when you meet the right one, the one that God has sent your way, that your heart is bigger than you ever imagined."

Izzy stood there on the outskirts of the crowd of sweet people she hadn't even entered yet, at the party she hadn't wanted to come to and here she stood having a conversation that struck hard... What, oh, what would it be like to have feelings or be loved like that? Oh, she didn't want to have that love and lose it. But to find love like that twice was a blessing. God had made a path and opened that up for this sweet woman, Pollyanna. It was like a song in her heart and Pollyanna's name fit well in a song and her grams were probably going to start singing again. And she wished they would, she missed the sound in the quiet.

"Thank you, Pollyanna, I've never loved anyone like that." *Really.* "But one day I hope to know love like you've described it."

Pollyanna placed a hand on her forearm and squeezed gently. "You will. And I have to tell you that sometimes it will surprise you. It could sneak up on you like it did me the second time. It can startle you, take you by the collar and make you think that you're doing the wrong thing, making the wrong choice or that it's not the dream you had. You know, there are some people who have had things happen to them before they fall in love. And that makes them think they don't want it."

Her words struck Izzy in the face, in the heart. *Luc.* She knew that was where he was now. "Thank you. I enjoyed our talk and am so glad you've been blessed to find love twice. Now, I need to go mingle before the ladies come hunt me down. They pretty much forced me to come no matter what."

Pollyanna grinned the biggest smile of the night. "Scared of their matchmaking?"

"Yes, I didn't come to Mule Hollow with plans to be matched and they know it."

"*That doesn't mean anything*," Pollyanna sang. "Believe me, there is proof walking around here about that. A lot, most of these smiling faces, came from matches made in heaven, not by the matchmakers. They just tweak a few things."

Izzy was amazed, this woman had a way about her. "I bet people love coming to your B&B and come back for more."

"They do. It's very busy. But I don't think it's me. It's that they can come to this wonderful town and join in on the dances or the programs we hold. But also," she chuckled, "I've got a cockatiel that likes to babble and some ornery goats for them to play with and a bunch of wrinkled puppies that love to jump and play before they're adopted by many of the people who come to stay at the inn. Please come out for coffee and to play one day."

"I will. How can I resist?" *So true.*

And then they hugged, and each walked away, each going to mingle with others. But Pollyanna's words, all of her words, did not leave Izzy's mind. And Luc was there in the headline of those thoughts.

Luc stood off to the edge of the party. He'd been moving a lot all evening and hoping that no one noticed. He was avoiding everywhere he saw Izzy heading.

"You sure have been moving around a lot," Chance Turner said.

The preacher had been watching him. "I have a lot of people to visit with, I'm sure you do too." Did it sound like he was trying to get the preacher to move on?

Chance grinned. "I do, but I don't know, I have this feeling that I'm supposed to be talking to you. You sing in the choir at church, and you come to most everything, and I noticed you don't participate as much as most people do. But I've noticed lately you've been acting a little bit more shut down. So, is there something going on?"

He was speechless, so he fought for what to say. "No." He'd just *lied* to the preacher.

Chance grinned again. "Okay, if you say so. But you know, I am the preacher, the pastor or just a guy that lives in the same town as you. The rodeo guy, dad of four kids now. You can call me whatever you want, but because I'm the pastor, no one else will ever know. Just wanted to let you know that. For some reason, God's put you on my mind and heart from the day you arrived in town. But I've just been watching and waiting, thinking you'd come to me. But you haven't and for some reason the last little while, I haven't stopped thinking about you. That Sunday you practically stormed out of church through the side door really put me on alert. Then today, watching you moving around almost as if you're hiding in dark corners brought me over. Made me know it was time for me to step up and put this out there."

He wanted to spin and walk away but he couldn't. And he needed to talk. And like Chance had just pointed out, he was the pastor and what Luc said was just between the two of them. And he believed him. He had a feeling he had a few new friends in town that if he told them, they wouldn't tell anyone either but, as he looked into the eyes of this ex-rodeo champ, rodeo preacher who'd come to Mule Hollow and taken the position as preacher of the church that needed him, he finally felt like he could share what was on his heart and mind.

Luc gave in. "Yeah, I am having some problems. You know Pace, he knew I needed some help, so he sent me here. He knew I wasn't looking for a wife and suddenly it's dawned on me that he sent me here because he sensed that I might talk to you."

"I hoped that he might think that. And I hope that you feel confident that it's between you and me. It's not even something I'd share with my sweet, amazing wife, and she understands that. If someone gives me permission to talk with her because they think she can help me, then she's in. She married me because she knew who I am and what my calling is. And that's talking with you right now. So where do you want to talk? Do you want to talk now or later?"

"Now. Because I don't want to—well, I don't want to say chicken out but that's kind of how I feel."

"Then come on, let's head over there to the far side where those two empty chairs are. People don't usually come bother me when they see me talking privately to someone."

Well, that was going to be rough. Everyone was going to know he was talking to the preacher. But so be it. His gaze slid across to where Izzy had her back to him as she was talking to a group of ladies. If he wanted to talk, now was the time. Maybe she wouldn't see him over there talking.

They crossed the grass to the area near the back of the yard and two chairs that weren't sitting next to each other but had a small table sitting between them. He wondered if Norma Sue had set it up for talks like this.

They each took a seat. He took the one where he'd be seen less—he was a big chicken. "So here is the deal." He then went on and spilled his story. About his family and losing them instantly. He'd driven because it gave him more control and yet he'd not been able to protect them, and he'd been in the seat that had survived when the big truck slammed into them. It just wasn't right.

He hadn't been able fix it or overcome it. And he spilled it all to the preacher man. Then he stopped talking.

"That was hard. I understand. I've been through some stuff and talked to a lot of people with problems. Feeling responsible is a terrible thing. And I'll say this because I've been in your shoes. I didn't stop a bull rider who shouldn't have been on the back of a bull, and I sensed it when he climbed onto the back of it. He didn't make it out alive, and I live with that every day. I had to give it over to the Lord, and He's led the way for me. But as you can tell, when God puts someone on my mind, I reach out. I don't rush, but there comes a time when I do the reaching. Tonight was one of those nights. So, talk to me, Luc. There are times that you can't overcome something or forget it, whether it was your fault or not. Feeling responsible isn't easy, but if you've asked God for forgiveness and God has done just that, it still doesn't take the pain away that you're feeling or the way you're hindering your life. But sometimes God sends things into your life to help you. To open your eyes. To show you the way."

Izzy.

Her name echoed through him in that moment. Was she the one sent to help him move forward?

"I know it wasn't my fault, But I still can't forget. I couldn't stop it from happening.

"No, you couldn't. Sometimes we don't understand why death happens to someone. We don't know what God is using it for or in some instances what God is protecting them from later in life. I'm just telling you we don't always know what God is dealing us or why or what blessing He's giving us or the person who died. But, what's He keeping you from?"

"I can't ever deal with losing anyone I love like that again. My fault or someone else's fault, or just God taking them when it's their time. I can't, so I've committed to staying single. When I met Pace, he knew I wasn't a loner like he used to be, but I was holed up out there on those humongous ranches that needed someone to take care of the cattle all alone when the hard, freezing winter came. I did it, but I'm pretty positive that God took me there after loner Pace had come to accept Him and knew that he wasn't meant to be hiding out in the solitude of the huge range. I was there just before he left and connected to him. I saw a loner meet the Lord and change his life by stepping out and coming to Mule Hollow. He met the town, Sheri, and now he trains horses all over the world and teaches others to do the same. And Sheri goes along with him. And while he does it, he's able to give his message and witness to people...

"Me included. He got me here to be around these people and, I am positive now, to talk to you. He knew I wasn't meant to be holed up like that for the rest of my life..." He didn't mention Izzy.

Izzy didn't want to stay here. Izzy wanted a different life. Izzy was just here because of her grams. If there was something between him and Izzy, even if he opened his heart...that didn't mean she would.

"And then what's come up? Like I said, I've been watching, and that first Sunday Izzy was here I saw something. I'm not sitting with my back to the choir. I'm sitting to the side, and I saw your face when you were singing "When We All Get To Heaven." When we all get to heaven it's going to be a glorious day. A happy day and an amazing day. And Izzy knows that. She has a whole family of grams waiting on her and more before them. But she just came here to bring them with her. To watch from above all the fun she's having here living life in the town just for them. But she's moving on, isn't she?"

"Yes, she is."

"And she's your neighbor."

"Yes, she is." Could this man read his mind?

"You know that house is where Sheri lived. Stubborn Sheri who wasn't looking for love when she rode into town with Lacy Brown. She'd already warned the matchmakers not to fix her up. Then your buddy Pace moved in down there at the end of the road. I'm just going to tell you that sometimes when God has a plan, it might not be your plan, but He knows what works. What's best for you. He knows how certain people are meant to bless each other. To work together. To make things happen. For His good. For their good. For everyone's good. When it's God's plan, it works. So, I'm going to get out of your way and let you enjoy the night. And hope I might have said something that doesn't just sting or aggravate you. But sometimes you have to let go, step out and take a chance on what God has planned for you. Not what you've decided is right for you. I had to do that. A lot of people have had to do it. But I'm just going to tell you when you go to Sam's and that jukebox gets stuck on "Pink Cadillac" and some of the other songs, odd, but they can touch your heart when you need them to."

Need them to. "Yeah, I get it. I hear songs in my head all the time and I don't know why. As weird as it sounds, I've been hearing *Green Acres* in my head. Out of all the songs to be hearing, I woke up with it blaring in my head and I don't know why."

Yes, you do. Izzy's grams sang it to her with Mule Hollow in the place of Green Acres.

Chance grinned. "Well, as a kid I enjoyed that show and those two not matched people. He wanted to live in the country, and she was a city girl. They found life together on *Green Acres*. You never know, maybe Mule Hollow is like that. Maybe there's a plan. And God's given you a nudge."

What?

Luc stared at Chance; his brain started thinking about all those green acres surrounding him since coming to Mule Hollow. And the woman who'd ridden a horse with him over those green acres that day. The woman who lived across those green acres in that little house.

His gaze shifted around, searching the area, but he didn't see Izzy.

He looked back at the preacher. "I never thought about it that way. But I like the green acres that are here, I like them a lot."

And maybe Chance was right, maybe God was telling him to step out of his comfort zone, let his guard down...but could he do that?

CHAPTER TWENTY-FIVE

Izzy had turned just in time to see Luc walk over to the far corner with Pastor Chance, and they were talking seriously.

Her heart trembled, and she prayed a quick, silent prayer that the preacher could help him. She couldn't help it, but she was leaving and she was aggravated and she was confused. She looked around at everyone and all the sweet people that she had met and would always love because she was leaving if she stayed with her plans.

It's your plans.

It struck her in that moment as her gaze flew back to Luc. His head was turned as he listened to what Preacher was saying. He was trying to take the blame for something that hadn't been his fault. He was fighting to keep his life simple, to never fall in love because he never wanted to hurt like that again. He didn't want to love anyone that he could lose if something happened. It was heart-touching.

Then here she was, it struck her like a fist to the gut. She was planning on leaving, no matter what. She had only come to Mule Hollow to fulfill her grams' dreams, but she had plans. She had plans to move to a city, she didn't even know which one, to open a salon and witness for God. And yet, here she was in this tiny little town, loving it, living her grams' dream, and now she knew she might be trying to avoid her future—her destiny?

Her heart thundered suddenly. She couldn't. Surely she wasn't avoiding God's plan for her life. Could she be the one that God used to help Luc?

Her heart raged at the thought. Suddenly it all made sense and she was overwhelmingly thankful it was her. Then, as if in answer, Norma Sue, Esther Mae, and Adela stood around her. And off to the side she got a grin from Lacy. She was playing with her kids on the ground and letting the clever Matchmakin' Posse of Mule Hollow take the lead. They had that *look* in their eyes—meaning no telling what was going on in their minds.

But suddenly it didn't matter. The question was, what was on her mind?

Izzy, you know what you want. Dreams change and God and your sweet grams got you here and for what?

And then Gram and Grammy started singing in heaven and her head again…and she smiled big as she listened to the words…

Mule Hollow is the place to be…

Meeting your match is a fun destiny…

You'll be there and so will he…

Don't let him get away…

Help him smile again…

Her smile grew as tears welled in her eyes, and she knew…

She might be here for her destiny, she was here to help Luc. God worked in mysterious ways sometimes and this time she was just going to let Him work.

"What's up, ladies?" she asked, her smile turning to

a grin as their eyes sparkled in the lights.

"Are you going to go ask your cowboy to dance?" Esther Mae asked.

"No, he's not my boyfriend." She wanted him now to be more than that.

Norma Sue hitched her brows and dipped her chin. "You know you like him, and more than that actually. You just don't want to admit it."

Yes she did but she teased them. "Norma Sue, Esther Mae, and Adela." She looked at each one of them. "What are y'all doing?"

Adela looked at her with those penetrating blue eyes of hers and gave a soft, gentle smile. "Darlin', we're trying to help you open up and know what's good for you. We just can't make that decision for you. But we can encourage you, and we know we're not your sweet grams, but we know they must have really wanted the right things for you. So, we're stepping in for them. We think that's what the Lord is wanting us to do."

"You ladies, the Matchmakin' Posse of Mule Hollow are wonderful. I loved my grams dearly and thank y'all for trying to be here when they can't be…"

Her words scrambled as tears surged up inside of her. "I feel awkward talking about it but Luc has some deep emotional troubles, and I just can't…"

What are you doing?

Heart twisting like a tornado, she gave up. "Okay, ladies, I'm trying not to talk because it's not my spot to do so. But I think I'm here for Luc. He's all I can think about. And I think he needs me."

All three ladies smiled huge, knowing smiles.

"It's wonderful that you see it now," Adela said gently. "Now, what are you going to do about it?"

Norma Sue hitched both brows.

And Esther Mae almost shook with excitement as she said voraciously, "Start with a dance."

Izzy sucked in a deep breath and knew, oh how she knew, yes she wanted to dance with Luc.

For the rest of her life if he wanted to dance with her. So, heart thundering, she stepped out determined to follow through and with the ladies watching, she strode straight toward him who held her heart.

Luc was looking around, as if searching for someone, and then his gaze locked onto her and he instantly took long strides toward her. They met near the edge of the dance floor. The music was playing, and she almost started crying, the emotions inside of her were so deep.

"I was trying to stay out of your way," she said, her words trembling.

He reached up and cupped her cheek, his hand warm and gentle. "I've been trying to stay away, drifting in and out around the area but keep you in my sights. But Izzy, I've talked to Chance and he helped me realize that I have to move forward. And the only forward I want is with you."

Joy burst through her. "Then we are in high agreement because all I want is you." She leaned her cheek into the touch of his palm, her gaze dropping to his lips, wanting to feel them on hers. "I didn't come here for this," she whispered.

"I didn't either. But I keep hearing this song playing in my head, and I just told the preacher that *Green Acres* with new verses and a different name of Mule Hollow had been playing in my head ever since you came into my life."

She laughed and tears began flowing. "Me too. My grams know how to sell something."

He pulled her into his arms then, *his* eyes glistening. "Yes, they do, darlin'. I don't know where in the world they got that kind of gift. That song is good, but this town is more important than *Green Acres* because, darlin', Mule Hollow is the place I found you. Mule Hollow is the place I want to start a new life over with you. And I can hear from heaven not only your grams cheering us on, but my family too. My dad, my mom, and my sister are singing too. We didn't need the matchmakers. We had our own matchmakers in heaven, and they've been getting into our hearts and brains."

"Oh yes they have," she agreed.

"I wake up in the morning with that song you sang, that your grams sang on my mind. Pastor Chance said, God has a way of working in very mysterious ways and it's true. Izzy, if you're in with me we're going to build our own *Green Acres* here in this community. We're going to move slowly, maybe, I know that what we've found between us hasn't moved slow at all. It's slammed into us like a hope-filled sunrise, and I'm thrilled about it."

"I am too. Startled, surprised, and amazed."

He grinned. "It's like when your grams and my family got together things started moving, and I'm not complaining." He hugged her against him, looking into her eyes.

Oh, how she loved this man.

"Izzy Cranberry, I, Luc Asher, love you with all my heart. You're everything I ever dreamed of and more—everything I shut away. With you, it's undeniable. So, I'm asking you right now, will you marry me?"

As if they were standing on stage with microphones, cheers erupted around them. They both took their eyes off of each other and glanced around. And sure enough, everything had stopped. The music had stopped, the dancing had stopped. The walking around and talking had stopped and everyone, including the head of the pack—the matchmakers of Mule Hollow—were standing there grinning and clapping.

And Izzy was smiling with all she had as she looked

back to the man holding her. "Luc Asher, you're making my dreams come true, so the answer is yes, I can't wait to marry you. I love you with all of my heart."

"And I love you too with all *my* heart. More heart than I even knew I had."

And then he kissed her. Laid those amazing lips that induced dreams in her heart, locked them together and kissed her.

Kissed her there in the place she hadn't known she dreamed of but her grams had. And she knew as long as she and Luc had together, their hearts would be locked together anywhere.

Not just Mule Hollow but wherever they were forever…

EPILOGUE

Izzy Cranberry was now Mrs. Luc Asher—she'd asked him if he wanted to become Mr. Cranberry and he'd said if it was the way to get her to marry him, he'd grinned and said, "I'll gladly be a Cranberry. They age really well and obviously remained faithful and love with all their hearts."

All true, but she'd hugged him and told him she was taking his name. And knowing her amazing Gram and Grammy were watching from above she looked toward heaven and smiled, God was good.

So good. She sighed with contentment just thinking about it and watched Luc across the reception tent surrounded by a herd of grinning cowboys. He'd found his place, not just in her heart but here among men, cowboys with hearts as big as Texas. It was perfect.

"Congratulations," Molly said, enthusiastically. "I just want to say my readers loved your romance and will love the addition about your beautiful wedding. Thanks for letting me get involved."

Grinning, Izzy hung her head to the side. "Are you kidding? My Gram and Grammy deserved to get every word you typed up about them. They loved it I'm sure. And I bet your readers are going to be singing, *Mule Hollow is the place to be…* for a long time."

Molly laughed. "I know I am. But that one there." She nodded toward a bright, smiling Lacy who was heading their way. "She had a song for Mule Hollow too. I'm wondering if that inspired your grams to find a song of their own?"

"Y'all talking about this amazing wedding or did I hear song in that process?" Lacy placed her pink-painted fingernails on her hips and tapped away.

"I was telling Izzy her grams tune of singing, *Mule Hollow is the place to be…*isn't the first song ringing in the air here in our town of love."

Lacy's smile flashed wide and bright. "My song

that rang and still rings in my head comes from the great old show about the Love Boat, you know…" She grinned then sang, *"Love is in the air and hair… Mule Hollow, where all your dreams come true…"*

They all laughed and then hugged and grinned at each other. *"This town,"* Izzy said with joy erupting inside of her. "Is the place to be. And songs, oh my goodness it is filled with songs. I'll always be singing and thankful my sweet grams got me here."

Norma Sue, Esther Mae, and Adela joined in on the hug.

"We're glad they did," Norma Sue said. "This is the place that wives will always be wanted for our cowboys. And we're glad you've joined the club."

And her gaze rested across the room to Luc who was grinning and watching her. Tears brimmed in her eyes. "Oh yes, I'm so happy to be a member of the 'Wives needed club,' and I'm in for helping others find the love I, *we*…all know exist."

And she was. *Love*, it was a wonder and with a full heart she excused herself from her club members and walked across the span and met Luc halfway. With a happy heart she stepped into his embrace and she was home. And her grams were singing...

Mule Hollow is the place to be... Love happens in the most wonderful way... Never give up and you'll one day meet...

The man of your dreams.

The love of your life...

And she had...and then she kissed him.

And her heart sang along with her grams...she was home.

Moments later, from across the way she caught the young Max watching them with a strange look on his face. A look she understood. "Luc, I think my grams might be singing in Max's head now. He's got that strange look on his face..."

Luc slid a glance Max's way then grinned back at her. "I think you're right. Oh boy, what a love show that will be."

She sighed. "Yes it promises to be. But, Luc, I love you and I'm so glad we get to be the star of our love story from here on in."

"Darlin', I am too. Come on, let's get this dance

started."

"Please, let's do. I'm so ready to dance with you."

And together they headed for the dance floor, songs already playing... But she was so focused on the man she loved that all she heard was the thundering of her heart as he took her in his arms and they danced. Together for always.

Don't miss the next book in the
Texas Matchmakers At It Again series—
THE TROUBLE WITH AN EVERLASTING COWBOY

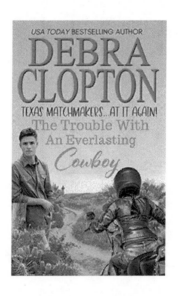

Welcome back to Mule Hollow for a romance that's sure to make you smile. No, it's not Bad, Bad Leroy Brown but like the old song there's trouble brewing and romance that won't go away...

Max Cantrell is building his Prickly Pear Jelly business he and his mom opened when they first came to Mule Hollow when he got off the bus at thirteen. Max is now twenty-five and zeroed in on expanding and going full speed ahead with the business. Then <i>she</i> rides into the prickly pears on her red motorcycle and turns his whole life into turmoil.

Lee Ann Brown's life has been bad, *really* bad even her name isn't her own. It's given to her because she had no name, no family just flung to the side like she was nothing. Now, after moving from family to family she's in control and her and her motorcycle are free and on their own. She's learned to take up for herself, enjoy life as she wants to and no one's messing with her. Yep, she's seeing the USA then the world one job and town at a time—until she has a flat in the middle of a prickly pear farm whose wild, beautiful colors drew her off-road.

And then, she sees him—the striking cowboy wrangling the prickly pears and his eyes turn to her and things she's not expecting erupt inside and the fight is on.

Welcome back to Mule Hollow where love is *still* in the air—and the prickly pears. The Matchmakin' Posse get that old song *Bad, Bad Leroy Brown* stuck in their heads and see a gal whose determined to live life her way. But God's got a plan and the Matchmakers are in on it full throttle.

And sweet-old-meddling Esther Mae wants a ride on the red motorcycle and plans to get it.

About the Author

Debra Clopton is a USA Today bestselling & International bestselling author who has sold over 3.5 million books. She has published over 81 books under her name and her pen name of Hope Moore.

Under both names she writes clean & wholesome and inspirational, small town romances, especially with cowboys but also loves to sweep readers away with romances set on beautiful beaches surrounded by topaz water and romantic sunsets.

Her books now sell worldwide and are regulars on the Bestseller list in the United States and around the world. Debra is a multiple award-winning author, but of all her awards, it is her reader's praise she values most. If she can make someone smile and forget their worries for a few hours (or days when binge reading one of her series) then she's done her job and her heart is happy. She really loves hearing she kept a reader from doing the dishes or sleeping!

A sixth-generation Texan, Debra lives on a ranch in Texas with her husband surrounded by cattle, deer, very busy squirrels and hole digging wild hogs. She enjoys traveling and spending time with her family.

Visit Debra's website and sign up for her newsletter for updates at: www.debraclopton.com

Check out her Facebook at: www.facebook.com/debra.clopton.5

Follow her on Instagram at: debraclopton_author

or contact her at debraclopton@ymail.com

Made in United States
Orlando, FL
26 October 2023

38277100R00157